TORRENTS

James P. Barber

Also by James P. Barber

The Blacksmith

Hill of the Bear

Recollections of a Museum Collector

The Collector, the Guide and the Bone Digger

The Gifted Way to Manage Your Career

The Hilgendorf-Haag Connection

From New York to Indiana:
A History of the Ira Barber Family Beginning in 1786

TORRENTS

James P. Barber

THE OTHER ROAD PUBLISHING

TORRENTS
The Other Road Publishing
630 Nancy Street, Warsaw, Indiana 46580
www.jamespbarber.com

Printed in the United States of America

First Edition, 2024

ISBN: 979-8-218-34516-7

Cover Design by James P. Barber

Other works by James P. Barber can be found at www.jamespbarber.com.

DEDICATION

This book is dedicated to my maternal great-grandfather, Louis (Ludwig) C. Wendt, who was the inspiration for this story. Louis, who was born Ludwig in Germany in 1850 or 1851, immigrated to America in 1882 at the age of thirty-one. With him were his wife and three small children. Living in La Porte, Indiana, Louis became a naturalized citizen in 1913.

The inspiration for the main character of this book came from a photograph of my great-grandfather. I do not have a date for the photograph, but I would guess him to be in his late-fifties in age.

Census records show that Louis was a night policeman, policeman, and watchman between 1900 and 1910. A note on the back of the picture indicates that, at the time of the photograph, he was one of three La Porte policemen.

I have no other information about his work in law enforcement. There are no other similarities to the main character of this book. The photograph simply inspired me to write a story about a policeman in the early 1900s.

ACKNOWLEDGMENTS

My wife Marti was the first person to read my first clean draft of the book. She is not an editor, a critic, or a bibliophile; however, I value her thoughts on my writing. I might call her an avid reader as she belongs to a local book club. My books are not always to her style, but I always appreciate her feedback. I can rely on her to be frank in her opinions. We may disagree, but I always take a second look at what she has to say. Thanks. I love you, dear.

The waves of death swirled about me;
*   the torrents of destruction overwhelmed me.*
The cords of the grave coiled around me;
*   the snares of death confronted me.*

In my distress I called to the Lord;
*   I called out to my God.*
From his temple he heard my voice;
*   my cry came to his ears.*

2 Samuel 22:5-7 (NIV)

CHAPTER 1

The space is quiet and brightly lit. Some might consider it intense and sterile with such an incredible radiance. The brightness, however, is not cold; there is a warmth to it that seems to allow a gentleness and a peace to flow throughout as it wraps the area. There is an aura of stillness, like the warmth of a perfect summer day with the most gentle of breezes.

Breaking up the bright whiteness of the room are fresh flowers. There are many large vases placed around the room filled with colorful, sweetly fragrant bouquets. Each unique arrangement offers an exceptional beauty against the white backdrop. New clusters of the freshly cut colorful blossoms are placed daily.

The air is filled with a low, harmonious, soothing sound that seems to emanate from the air itself rather than from any other source. The sound enfolds every presence with an incredible sense of wonder. It is as if a quiet voice is speaking and singing at the same time. It is all a part of the environment meant to assure complete calm, even when tumultuous events may be in the offing.

Michael spoke with complete and unquestionable authority, as confirmed by his position. He did not laud his authority over the one with whom he was meeting. There was no need for him to do so. They each knew their individual role, each accepting without question their respective stations. The order of their positions made their missions that much easier with a clarity of commission. And besides, they were all there to serve the one indisputable leader. That was the ultimate duty of each of them.

Michael had been entrusted with carrying out the directive as it had been decided by the Council. The Council members had listened with care to the guidance that had been provided to them. All perspectives had been considered within the three tiers of the Council. Of course, the leader could overrule them all, but he was always willing to listen to their recommendations.

After appropriate deliberation, there had been no dissension on the matter at hand. The elite members of the Council were all in agreement. Michael was selected to see that the decision of the Council was carried out.

Michael called in a messenger who would be in direct control of the assignment. The messenger had one goal, and that was to deliver the ruling of the Council.

Michael began, "I have a new assignment for you. Yours is one Felsen Krieger of Western New York State." Michael revealed to the messenger how the Council had ruled regarding the target. The messenger was allowed to fully understand the reasoning of the Council. He was not, however, allowed to question even the most minor aspect of the decision.

Michael continued explaining all the details regarding Felsen Krieger and his family. No notes were taken, as the messenger was expected to retain every detail. The messenger's training and experience assured this goal would be met. It was not the place of either Michael or the messenger to judge anything about the man. Their duty was to carry out the Council's assignment, which they had done many times before, and would dutifully do so once again. Michael provided all the specifics, and the messenger listened with rapt attention to assure nothing was missed.

As the meeting ended, the messenger reviewed every piece of information provided. To him, it was like a beautifully orchestrated piece of music. Still, he was given the latitude to make determinations on how to approach the details of the assignment. The trust and empowerment he was given encouraged him. He would ensure that the results desired by the Council would be fully achieved. Nothing less was to be expected.

CHAPTER 2

Marie looked up and smiled at Fels as she placed her fork on the empty plate in front of her. "Felsen, I hope you are not going to ride that foul motor bicycle down to the tavern." Marie used his full name when she wanted to feign anger with Fels. She was emphatic, but she was not upset that Fels might ride his motorcycle to the tavern to get a newspaper. She just did not like Fels' preferred mode of transportation. To her, it was loud and dangerous. The bicycle seemed a much safer and more neighborly means to get about town.

Fels had purchased the 1913 Harley-Davidson motorcycle two years ago. He had revived it from its winter rest in the former milk barn behind their house in the late spring. It took most of an entire Saturday to get it into running condition. He enjoyed tinkering with the thing. His time working on the motorcycle allowed his mind to detach from the often harsh realities of his job. By summer, he was enjoying the daily trip to work on his favorite form of transportation.

It was an unseasonably cool and clear July day, and Fels had planned for a short evening walk after dinner. For a moment, he felt challenged by Marie's comment.

He quickly tossed that feeling aside, walked across the dining room to his smiling wife, gently wrapped his hands around her thin waist, and kissed her on the cheek. The children, still seated at the table, giggled.

"Marie, my dear, it is a wonderful evening for a walk. I will not be riding my motorcycle, or the, uh, 'motor bi-cycle' as you call it." Fels chuckled. He adored the way she sometimes mixed her words when talking about things she did not fully understand.

"Whatever you call that beastly thing, I'm just glad you won't be riding it." Her smile warmed as she looked into Fels' eyes. She reached up and touched his cheek with her hand. "And, you are right, it is a beautiful evening for a walk." The love they shared extended that brief glance into a pure moment of deep and everlasting bliss for both of them.

As Marie and the children began clearing the dinner table, Fels grabbed his hat and started toward the front door of their modest home. They had purchased the home almost a year ago with the financial backing of Marie's father. Fels had not wanted to rely on Mr. Kurz's help, but Marie had insisted. Saying no to Marie was dif-ficult for Fels.

Marie called after him as he put on his hat. "Oh, Fels, I meant to let you know that Central Coal brought our delivery yesterday. He told me we were saving money by making our purchase in mid-summer like this."

"Good. That's as I expected. We should be set for our heating needs into this fall. Saving a little money never hurts."

"You enjoy your walk. Children, come help me wash the dishes." Marie rounded up eleven-year-old Ludwig and nine-year-old Frieda and ushered them into the kitchen. "We'll have everything finished by the time your father returns."

Fels turned, smiled at the children, and threw them a kiss. "I won't be long."

After he left the house, Fels turned right and proceeded toward Oliver Street, where Reeg's Tavern was located, just about three blocks away. It was a friendly neighborhood tavern that served coffee, sandwiches, and drinks. Fels had never known of a problem with disorderly drunks at the establishment. People seemed to enjoy themselves with a quiet bite to eat and some good German draft beer. After a long week of hard labor for most of them, it was a nice place to relax.

The air was cooling as the sun lowered to the west. When Fels found himself walking at his normal quick pace, he consciously forced himself to slow down. He had had a demanding day at the police department wrapping up an investigation into a string of burglaries. A detective's duties meant more cases, more hours, and more reports to complete, as Fels had discovered four years ago with his promotion.

Fels observed that the small-time gangs of thieves were getting younger in age. He thought of his own children. He and Marie were doing everything they could to ensure that Ludwig and Frieda would grow into intelligent, hard-working contributors to the good of modern society. They wrapped the children with their love and taught them early to walk with the Lord. Setting their hearts right was the key to building solid lives.

Fels turned left onto Oliver Street and walked less than half-a-block to Reeg's Tavern. A few men at the bar looked up as Fels passed through the doorway. He recognized most of the faces. They were not friends, or even acquaintances, just various people he knew from the general area of the neighborhood. Fels assumed most of them knew he was in law enforcement, and they chose not to make an appearance of being familiar with him. Fels wanted law enforcement to be a trustworthy and reliable source of aid in times of need, making this a heavy burden on him. But it seemed most people perceived the force as being dedicated to catching them doing something wrong. They looked with suspicion at an officer of the law.

Fels stopped at a small set of shelves just inside the entrance. It usually sat outside the door on the sidewalk, but Jacob, the owner, always had it brought inside in the evening near sunset.

Fels picked up a copy of the *Buffalo Daily Courier* for July 28, 1915, and scanned the front page. Nearly a year had passed since Great Britain had entered the war with Germany. Stories of the war efforts from around the world dominated all the current news. Germany, Great Britain, Italy, Japan, and even South American countries all appeared in prominence in the printed headlines. The British had declared a blockade of all German ports, but more recent events were straining German relations with the United States. President Wilson was keeping the United States out of the war, a position with which Fels was in agreement. But, recent events were pressing for American involvement. The headline in today's paper read, "Future of Friendly Relations Put Squarely Up to Germany In Draft of *Lusitania* Note." The sinking of the British ocean liner *Lusitania* had occurred in May, killing 1,198 passengers, including 128 United States citizens.

As quickly as he had scanned the front page of the newspaper, Fels put the war thoughts behind him. He folded the newspaper, placed it under his left arm, and stepped over to the bar. He had only one cigar left in his coat pocket, and he needed to refill his cigar case. The cigars were the more important reason, rather than the newspaper, for Fels' evening stroll.

Fels raised his right arm to get the attention of the barkeeper. "Hello, John," he hailed, with a smile on his face. The barkeeper looked up at Fels and headed his way. Fels held out his hand as John approached. They shook hands in a warm, friendly manner.

"So, Jacob's not working again tonight?" Fels said.

The barkeeper knew Fels well and was a friendly sort. Fels was a solid friend to Jacob, the owner, and John knew that. Jacob wanted to have a good relationship with Fels in case of trouble at his tavern. But, law enforcement or not, Jacob truly liked Fels. And besides, there had been no time when Jacob needed to call the law to his establishment.

John leaned forward on the bar with both hands. "No, he's still under the weather. What can I get for you, Detective Krieger? Would you like a beer this evening?"

Fels had never mentioned his exact position or his promotion to detective to anyone at the tavern, including John. Simply being an officer of the law to those in the tavern was just fine with him. He saw no need to appear to be boastful about his position. Fels was truly a kind and humble man at heart. However, he could also be firm and intimidating when it was required on the job.

Fels took the paper from under his arm and placed it on the bar. "No, thanks. I just need some cigars and the newspaper."

"Sure. Still smoking the Aristocrats?"

"Yes. That'll do just fine. Give me five of the straights."

John retrieved the cigars and placed them on the bar in front of Fels. "So, that's five cigars at five cents each and the newspaper. That'll be twenty-six cents."

Fels counted out his change and paid John. "Thanks, John. You have a good evening."

John tipped his head to Fels. "You too, detective."

Fels retrieved his cigar case from his coat. It was nicer than anything he would ever have bought for himself, but Marie had given it to him on his twenty-fifth birthday. It was an English alligator case with sterling silver trim on the lid. Fels thought of Marie every time he opened it.

While she was not entirely fond of his cigar smoking, Marie tolerated it and could see how much Fels enjoyed it. She did notice how Fels relaxed when he took the time to smoke a cigar. And she had to admit to herself that the aroma, when fresh, was not all that bad. The stale smell of burned out cigars, however, was not to her liking.

Fels took the one lone cigar out of the case and re-filled it with the five fresh cigars. He admired the aroma of the cigars before closing the case and returning it to the vest pocket of his coat. He tapped the outside of his coat after replacing the case.

Fels stepped through the door and out onto the side-walk, pulled a match out of his vest, and struck it on the brick wall of the building. He bit off the end of the cigar and spit the tobacco past the curbing of Oliver Street. He puffed on the cigar to get the tobacco burning. After sev-eral short drafts, the cigar was lit, and Fels enjoyed the first full draft.

With the newspaper tucked tightly under his arm, Fels began his walk home. He was unaware he was walk-ing in a more relaxed manner than he had been earlier. Fels looked up at the first bright stars in the clear, dark-ening sky and admired them. He thought of his family and the joy they brought to him. His work was hard, his hours were long, his days were mostly frustrating, but at the end of each day, his family brought him warmth and joy.

Memories of joyful times with Marie and the children unexpectedly filled his head. As though a series of photo-graphs was passing before his eyes, Fels saw the chil-dren's births and baptisms, playful picnics, kites flying, and comfort being provided when they took a tumble. To top it all off, Marie was more caring of a mother than

Fels could ever have imagined. She had so much more patience with the children than he did, something he was finally learning, however, thanks to Marie's example. She had helped him to grow so much as a father and husband. He could not imagine the type of person he would have been without her. At the moment, Fels felt his love for his family deep in his soul. He was glad.

Fels exhaled a long draft from his cigar and watched the aromatic smoke rise in the night air. A shooting star flashed quickly across the sky. A dog barked in the distance. Fels fully realized his blessings and smiled to himself.

A loud thunderous boom shattered the still night air and awakened Fels' quiet mind. Fels stopped in his tracks and tilted his head. He saw the sky light up in the distance, and an instant later, he sensed a slight tremor under his feet. The light in the distant sky filled with a large billow of smoke. Fels immediately recognized that there had been a massive explosion.

The newspaper fell to the sidewalk from beneath his arm. He realized the explosion had come from the direction of his own home to the east. Fels pulled the cigar from his mouth and threw it to the ground. Thinking that he might need to provide assistance to someone in his neighborhood, Fels picked up the pace in the blast's direction.

Just over a minute later, Fels saw splinters of timbers scattered about and a flaming inferno where his house should have been. Stunned, Fels stopped, frozen in his tracks. His eyes darted left and right. *What's happening?!*

For a moment, it seemed as if time stood still. Fels willed his legs to carry him forward. He ran straight toward the blaze. Nearing the flaming remains of his house, Fels called out for Marie and the children. He looked about, expecting to see his family as a crowd gathered. He called out again several times. And, again, no reply. Onlookers stared with open mouths and began backing away as the flames grew higher.

Fels ran straight to the fire, but the heat and rising flames turned him back. He looked into the crowd, and once again, called out for his family. He ran to nearby onlookers, neighbors, asking if they had seen his family. He only received shaking heads with blank stares or quiet, downcast eyes.

Turning to the house, Fels' eyes briefly connected with those of a young man. For a moment, Fels felt as though he and the young man were in some manner connected. Fels' mind quickly returned to his dilemma. Feeling that he must act, Fels pushed past the young man standing in his path and entered what remained of the large front porch. He tried to reach the front entry, but the heat and flames drove him away from the engulfed door. He sought entry through a nearby broken window, but a wall of fire turned him back there as well.

Onlookers were shouting at him, but he did not hear them. Suddenly, the roof of the front porch collapsed on Fels. A large burning timber swung down from above and knocked him to one end of the porch. While Fels was lying there, another burning timber fell on his legs. At nearly the same moment, the young man he had pushed past just moments earlier pulled Fels from the porch just as it fully collapsed into flame. The young man patted Fels' clothing down, smothering the fire. He then dragged Fels away from the blazing inferno.

The fire continued to roar in the night. Sparks from the wooden structure drifted high into the night sky, appearing as if they were stars. Fels was completely unaware of anything at this point as he lay lifeless on the ground.

CHAPTER 3

Coughing, moaning, sobbing, metal clanging against metal, and multiple voices blended together in one unrecognizable dull sound that hammered inside Fels' head. None of it made any sense to him. He felt trapped in a dream from which he could not awaken. He could not put a thought together. The cacophony made it impossible to concentrate. *If only that sound would stop, I could think!*

He realized his eyes were closed. *I need to open my eyes. Why can't I do that?* His inability to understand his situation agitated him. *Open ... eyes!*

He lifted his uncooperative, heavy eyelids, but he was no less confused. *Where am I?* He looked around with blurred vision, his eyes stabbed by bright lights. He opened and closed his eyes several times to clear them, but that action provided only limited improvement. His head throbbed with a deep ache. He tried to sit up, but pain stung throughout his body. His head pounded all the more.

A vivid memory suddenly flashed through his head. He saw a blazing inferno. *Yes, there was a fire!* He heard the explosion in his mind. *It wasn't just a fire. There was an explosion!* His eyes darted about. He realized he was in the hospital. *Yes, I was injured ... but Marie and the children?!*

He needed answers, and he wanted them now. Fels called out for assistance. He continued screaming for help until a nurse rushed to his side.

"Tell me, please, where are my wife and children—a boy and a girl? Where are they?! I want to see them!" Agitated, he again tried to raise himself in the bed, but the pain was too intense. Falling back, his eyes widened as his thoughts cleared, but he remained unable to make sense of the situation.

"Settle down, Mr. Krieger. I'll get the doctor for you." Saying nothing more, she turned to leave.

Fels reached out and grabbed her arm. "Please tell me where my family is! Are they alright?" His tone was now more pleading than demanding.

The nurse saw the hurt in his eyes and his need for answers, but all she could do was again tell Fels she would get the doctor. Then she turned, and her quick footsteps on the tiled floor were like blows to Fels' pounding head.

For several minutes, Fels recalled more of what had taken place. He had gone out for a newspaper. It was evening, a beautiful evening. It was interrupted by an explosion, and the fire. He could not, however, remember anything that had happened to himself. He was unaware of how he had received his injuries or how severe they were. When Marie arrived, he was certain she could explain it to him. Fels expected her to walk in with the doctor at any moment. He closed his eyes in an attempt to block out the confusion he was experiencing. His mind was a whirlpool of images and thoughts that just would not coalesce.

Fels could not determine how much time had lapsed as his head continued throbbing. He briefly opened his eyes but quickly closed them again, attempting to shut out the pain. With no relief, Fels responded as the doctor arrived—alone. He was a tall, middle-aged, slim man. His thinning gray-brown hair was neatly combed. Fels did not recognize him, but he knew he must have the answers.

"Where is my wife? Will she be coming soon? Does she know I'm here? How soon can I leave?" Fels fired off the questions in rapid succession.

"There now, Mr. Krieger. I'll answer all of your questions in due time." He paused for only the briefest moment to be certain he had Fels' attention. "I'm Dr. Bellamy. I've been taking care of you since your arrival. Now, I need to see how you're doing. May I do a quick examination and ask you a few questions?" His tone was kind while insistent.

"But, my family?"

"We need to get you evaluated, then we'll talk. Okay?" The doctor did not wait for Fels to reply. "Now, tell me, how does your head feel?"

"It feels like I've been kicked by a cow; no, two cows ... and they're still kicking."

Dr. Bellamy removed a flashlight from his pocket. "I'm going to examine your eyes. Follow the light, please."

The first flash of the light painfully pierced his eyes, but Fels adjusted after blinking several times. Fels had no trouble following the doctor's flashlight as it was moved back and forth before his eyes. The doctor stopped the light and peered into Fels' eyes. Nothing in his demeanor or expression gave Fels any sense of the results of this examination.

The doctor then took Fels' right hand in his own. It was at that moment that Fels realized his left arm was in a cast. Fels was beginning to realize the extent of the injuries that he must have incurred in the explosion.

"Now, squeeze my hand." Fels complied. "Very good, Mr. Krieger."

"Can I get some answers now?" Fels' eyes tightened as his forehead tensed and wrinkled.

"Just a few more things." The doctor moved to the end of the bed and lifted the blankets covering Fels' feet. He ran a finger from Fels' heel to his toes on his left foot. "Do you feel this?"

"Yes." Fels was quick to answer, as he was eager to get this over with.

"Wiggle your toes for me."

Fels did as instructed.

"Very good."

The doctor repeated the process on Fels' right foot, and the results were the same.

Dr. Bellamy looked Fels straight in the eyes, waited for Fels to make eye contact, and then he spoke. "Mr. Krieger, you suffered a severe head injury, your left arm is broken, and your right leg is badly bruised from your hip to your foot. You have two cracked ribs. You have other cuts, scrapes, and bruises, as well as a few burns on your hands, arms, and face." The doctor paused, but not long enough for Fels to make any comments. "Now then, Mr. Krieger, tell me what you remember about what happened to you."

"I remember an explosion and a fire. Where's my family?!"

"I'm sorry, Mr. Krieger." The doctor paused and looked at Fels with compassion. "They did not survive the explosion."

"But ... wait. What do you mean?" Fels was confused and panicked.

"Mr. Krieger, your wife and children were killed."

"No, that can't be!" Stunned, Fels sat up and stared into space, ignoring the pain this time. "No! Why are you telling me this?!"

"Calm down, Mr. Krieger." The doctor tried to lower Fels onto his back, but Fels refused to lie back down.

"Don't tell me to calm down! What happened?! I remember an explosion. Tell me what happened!"

"Mr. Krieger, I am very sorry for your loss. The police have been investigating for nearly a week."

Fels interrupted, "A week?!" Fels' eyes darted back and forth as he tried to make sense of what he was hearing.

"Yes, you've been unconscious for six days now. It is what we call a carus, or coma. You are very fortunate to be alive. Coma patients often never recover from their deep sleep."

Fels was once again stunned beyond belief. "I want to know what they've learned. I want answers!" Fels fell into his law enforcement persona. It was who he would remain until he determined what had happened to his family.

"I'm afraid I don't have that information." The doctor was trying to keep the situation calm.

"Well, contact Chief Orville Bruckhart at the 5th Precinct and get him down here! I need to know what happened!"

Fels fell back in his bed exhausted, sweating, and hurting all over. Tears filled his eyes, not from the pain of his injuries, but from the pain of his loss. He closed his eyes, turned his head to the side, and sobbed.

"I'll have a nurse bring you something for the pain and something to settle you down." The doctor placed a consoling hand on Fels' shoulder, then left his bedside. Fels heard nothing and felt nothing but heartbreak.

Later that afternoon, Police Chief Orville Bruckhart from Tonawanda's 5th Precinct came into Fels' hospital room. Fels' head was on the pillow, turned away from the doorway, when Chief Bruckhart entered the room. Unsure if Fels was sleeping, he leaned in close to Fels and whispered, "Fels?"

Slowly turning his head, Fels looked into the chief's eyes. As his eyes filled with tears, Fels pleaded, "Chief ... what ... happened?"

Fels had worked under Chief Bruckhart at the 5th Precinct in Tonawanda for six years when Chief Bruckhart was the precinct captain. Through those years, Fels and Bruckhart had become close friends. The two remained close friends after Bruckhart had been promoted to the position of Chief of Police.

"Fels, I'm so sorry." There was a long pause. The chief looked down at the floor, but then he lifted his head and looked straight into Fels' eyes. He knew Fels well enough to know that Fels wanted the whole truth of what had happened.

"Fels, someone blew up your house with a charge of dynamite. The explosion appears to have originated near the rear of your house just off the alley. From what we can tell, they placed the dynamite near your coal chute, creating an explosion with all the greater magnitude. Fels, the rear half of your house was gone in an instant. Then fire spread rapidly to the rest of the house."

The chief paused again to let what he had said sink in. Fels stared in disbelief. The panic was gone as Fels now fully comprehended what he had been told.

"Marie was washing dishes with the children ... at the rear of the house ...." His voice trailed off. The emptiness he felt was beyond comprehension for him. He had truly lost a part of his very being.

"Fels, they didn't suffer. The force of the explosion killed them instantly." The chief tried to provide some consolation to Fels.

"Their bodies?" Fels was compelled. "I need to see them."

The chief looked down at the floor again. "Fels, I'm sorry, there was little in the way of remains."

Fels sobbed. Chief Bruckhart sat next to him on the bed. Fels wrapped his right arm around the chief. Bruckhart pulled him in closer and held him. No words were spoken between the two men.

Fels wished he had been killed that night. What was the point of going on without his family? There was nothing left. His spirit was crushed.

CHAPTER 4

Over the next several days, Fels endured increased pain as his body awakened. Consciousness was intermittent as his mind coped with the pain and grief he suffered. His restless thoughts drifted to Marie, their courtship, and their marriage.

It seemed like only yesterday that Fels courted and then married Marie. They met at the Lutheran Church in Bergholz where Fels' great-grandfather, Friederich Roloff, had been a pastor after immigrating to America from Germany in 1844. Fels' grandfather, Ernst Krieger, worked a farm near Bergholz where Fels' own father was born. His father worked that same farm until he bought his own property about ten miles southeast of Bergholz. It was there, in a close-knit German community, that Felsen Krieger was born to Ludwig and Johanna Krieger in 1886.

Fels worked hard on that farmstead with his family, but he always knew there was something else for him beyond the farm. He tinkered with the farm implements as he had a strong desire to know how tools and machinery were built and how they accomplished their express purposes. He even tried making a few changes to some of the equipment to improve upon its function. That, unfortunately, did not always sit well with his father. In his father's eyes, Fels was wasting time that would be better utilized by working in the fields and helping with the livestock. His father was a driven taskmaster with little tolerance for idleness or for activities he did not feel were productive.

Fels was close to his mother as a child. Fels enjoyed reading, which his mother encouraged. She was proud that, of their five children, Fels took the most interest in books and reading. And since his father spoke German regularly, Fels picked up both languages and would often read the German newspapers that his father read. However, Fels was never allowed to read the paper until his father was finished with it. The paper's place on a small table next to his father's chair meant it was not to be touched.

Ludwig Krieger had insisted that his family speak the German language at home. While he was an American by birth, Ludwig was insistent that they not lose their German roots, something his own father had demanded. He was a proud man, and he was proud of the hard work ethic of the German people. It was what his father and grandfather had taught him, and it would be no different for his own family. He viewed it as his duty as the head of his family. He felt the richness of the German tradition as it had been taught to him. Beyond seeing it as a duty, he saw it as loyalty to his father.

At home with the family, Fels enjoyed working on puzzles with his mother. He welcomed every challenge of increasingly complex puzzles. His mind was keen at visualizing patterns, not only in the puzzles, but more importantly, in the improvements Fels worked on with the farm equipment. It was a talent that was lost to Fels' father. Such inquisitiveness was a waste of good time in his father's eyes. Working the farm was always foremost to his father. Everything else was a mere extravagance that could only lead to a waste of valuable resources and appear to others as laziness, as sloth, that was forbidden by the Bible.

His father used the Bible as a tool to teach his children. He seemed to hold fast to the adage about sparing the rod and spoiling the child. It was his application of Proverbs 13:24, "He that spareth his rod hateth his son: but he that loveth him chasteneth him betimes." His father had a way of interpreting and applying the words in the manner that suited his personal wants and needs.

While Fels could foresee a day when he would leave the farm, he enjoyed being able to explore the land surrounding the farm ground itself. He appreciated the property and the wildlife within it at an early age. Fels especially enjoyed spending free time at a pond on the northern edge of the property. He poked around the muskrat huts and beaver dams, and studied the birds, frogs, snakes, and crawdads. The pond was located just under a half-mile northwest of the farmhouse. When he was done with his chores, Fels often set out over a low rolling hill and headed for the pond.

On one particular day, Fels had just finished milking the cows, put away the milk buckets, and left the barn for the pond. It was a cool fall day with just enough sunshine to provide a little warmth on his cheerful face. Nearing the pond, Fels picked up a long stick. He could use it to probe the muddy bottom along the shore to see what he might stir to life. He also liked to poke in the muskrat huts to see if he could send any muskrats scurrying into the dark waters of the pond.

It was not a small pond, and so provided plenty of opportunity for Fels. He walked along the western edge of the pond, heading north. Grasses and weeds grew long near the pond, turning into rows of cattails in the lowland bordering the pond. There was a small bit of land jutting out into the pond on the north shoreline. Fels approached this finger of land. It was a bit higher than the land surrounding the pond, but it was well-soaked from recent rains. Fels expected his rubber milking boots would keep him dry enough, however.

The boy approached a muskrat hut at the farthest point of the saturated finger of land. He probed with his stick as he moved further toward the waters of the pond itself. As he waded into the pond, his right leg sank deep, filling his boot with water. This caused Fels to lose his balance and tumble sideways into the black water and thick mud. He reached out with his right arm as he fell, and it plunged through the water and into the mud.

The muck beneath the water sucked his arm in, and it went deeper into the boggy bottom. He had fortunately taken a deep breath before his face hit the surface of the water. He was now struggling to pull his right arm free. Instantly, he realized he could not move his right leg. His realization quickly turned to a great fear. *I'm going to drown!* he screamed in his head.

His fear became panic, and as Fels struggled harder, his arm and leg only became more deeply entrenched in the quicksand-like muck. He was now lying on his side at the bottom of the murky water. With his left hand, Fels wildly searched for his stick. He grasped about, his hand occasionally popping out just above the surface. His lungs burned. His fingers touched the stick just as he felt himself about to lose consciousness. At that moment, an amazing calm came over him, and he slipped into darkness.

Fels awoke lying on his side over a mound of dry grass near the north shore of the pond. He coughed and expelled a throat full of dirty water. As he coughed a few more times, he became aware of a figure towering over him. The bright sky above created a silhouette of the person.

The young man stared down at Fels and asked how he felt. Fels sputtered a bit and said, "I ... I think I'm okay." He was puzzled. Looking about his surroundings, he realized that he was soaked. "What happened?"

"I saw you go under in the pond. I got to you as quickly as I could. Your hand was tightly grasping your walking stick, but you were sucked into the mucky bottom of the pond."

Fels cleared his head and recalled the circumstances. "I thought I was a goner for sure."

"Well, you were in trouble. I was fortunate to see you."

Fels shaded his eyes to see the man's face. He noticed he was smiling. "Gee, thanks, mister."

Fels sat up. He saw the boot was missing from his right foot. He looked up at the man and said, "My father won't be happy about me losing my boot. They're my milk boots."

"Oh, don't worry, I was able to recover your boot." The young man held up the boot and handed it to Fels.

"Gosh, thanks, again, mister."

Fels stood and felt himself to make sure he was okay. He was only cold, wet, and muddy. After a few more coughs, he finally cleared the last bit of water from his lungs. He shivered, partly because of the cold and partly because of the realization that he had come close to losing his life.

"It looks like you're going be just fine." The young man spoke gently, "Be more careful next time." He smiled at Fels and held out his hand.

As Fels shook the man's hand, a warm calmness fell over him. He realized he was lucky to be alive, and that it was this person who had saved him. This man had given Fels a gift that he now felt in his heart.

The man nodded his head in the direction of the farmhouse. "You better head home and get out of those wet clothes."

"Would you like to come with me? My mother could get you something to eat, I suppose." Fels was unsure how to offer some gesture of thanks to the man. He did not recognize him from any of the nearby farms. Fels didn't even think to ask him what he was doing out by the pond.

"No, thanks. I'll just be on my way." The man smiled at Fels and turned to the northwest.

As the man walked away, Fels felt it odd that the man's clothes were already dry while he himself was still soaking wet. Fels tossed that thought aside and yelled to the man, "Hey, mister, what's your name?"

He called back, "I'm David," and he disappeared into a small grove of trees.

Fels headed home, knowing he would have to explain his soaked and muddy clothes. He would offer up that he fell near the edge of the pond ... but with none of the details.

CHAPTER 5

Ludwig Krieger, to the dismay of his own father, stopped attending the Lutheran Church in Bergholz. The family found another Lutheran Church in North Tonawanda not too far from the farm. German families would often gather after church services for a feast to which all contributed. It was easy for Ludwig to make friends with the men at these gatherings, and he enjoyed the fine German beer that he heavily consumed. Ludwig enjoyed talking of Germany and speaking German with these men. It was at these gatherings that Fels had seen his father laugh, something that was discouraged at home.

Fels enjoyed his Sunday friends. They ate, played games, teased the girls, and generally relaxed. Farm work and schooling occupied Fels all the other days of the week. Growing up on a farm left little time for anything besides farm labor. There were morning chores before school, afternoon chores following school, and evening chores before bedtime. Saturdays were devoted to the farm. During harvest season, school was sacrificed in order to gather the crops. Of course, animals needed tending on Sunday just as on any other day of the week.

But time at church was time away from the farm, and a welcomed occasion to Fels.

So, Fels came to appreciate his time at church. His inquisitive mind became engaged, and in no time at all, he found himself listening intently and seeking clarification in the Bible. The idea of an eternal life in heaven had its appeal to him. He was discovering the message of love and forgiveness as taught by Jesus. He was learning about mercy and grace and repentance. A valuable teaching for Fels was the importance of having a servant's heart. Not all of it made complete sense to him in his youth, but it was building a solid foundation for his future.

Fels volunteered to help some of the younger children with their Sunday school activities. He continued this involvement as he grew older. It was while assisting with the other children that he met Marie. She was nearly two years younger than Fels, but she could easily match him in knowledge of the Bible. They grew closer as they brought their small groups of students together for some fun activities. The two would discuss the day's sermon while the children played. Marie displayed a knowledge and a strength that Fels grew to appreciate.

Fels learned that Marie's father, Jacob Kurz, owned a clothing store in Buffalo. Marie had helped her parents in the store since she was a child. Shortly after meeting Fels, Marie was working at the store on a regular basis as a milliner, using her creative talents to design and fabricate ladies' hats. She was also well-organized and helped with shelving the store's goods. Fels couldn't help but admire her many gifts, one of which was making the somewhat shy boy feel comfortable when he was with her.

Their attraction to one another must have been a case to prove that opposites attract. While their work with the younger children at the church was something they had in common, most of their other characteristics appeared to be a study of contrasts.

Marie was what one might refer to as a refined woman. Both of her parents had seen to that. She always dressed well—with a very fashionable hat, of course. She was polite and quite pleasant. While she always presented herself in the best possible light, she was never ostentatious. She took pride in how she maintained herself, but she was never proud in her character. She was a humble person with every reason not to be. The younger children in her church group adored Marie.

Marie believed in the Golden Rule as taught by Jesus in his Sermon on the Mount in the Gospel of Luke, "And as ye would that men should do to you, do ye also to them likewise." She had a pure heart, and she was a warm, caring, and giving individual, always thinking of others before herself. She had a gift that enabled her to draw out the best in others, including Fels.

But Fels ... well, he was a farm kid. His clothes and looks were not of great interest to him. His mother had to prod him to get himself looking presentable for church. She had to remind Fels to clean the dirt from his boots before leaving the house on Sunday mornings. His hair was generally mussed, and his mother would try to improve it by running her fingers through his hair as they entered the church, something that embarrassed Fels.

Not a lot seemed to disturb Fels, though. He persevered at whatever activity he was undertaking, always expecting to succeed without fail. He did not like to be defeated. When he became focused on the task before him, he would get lost in it and block out everything, and everyone, else. In his mind, he was visualizing and organizing his thoughts. He would often carry a notepad and a pencil to jot down his ideas. Being logical made sense to Fels.

Marie's mother had died about a year before Fels met Marie. Marie's favorite keepsake was a hair comb that had belonged to her mother. It seemed to provide her with comfort and strength when she wore it. Its sentimental value was priceless to her. Like so many things with Marie, it was quite nice without being showy or extravagant.

Fels' favorite item was his pocket knife. His father had given it to Fels when he was six years old. Fels treasured that knife. He used it for its purpose as a tool, and he always took good care of it. The stag-handled knife had been made by a German company, and his father had told him it was far superior to any knife made by the Americans. At the age of six, Fels trusted and believed every word his father said.

Fels supported the farm with all of his strength, and with all of his father's expectations of him, but it was not what he wanted for his future. Fels' uncle Fred, who worked on the Rochester police force, had influenced him. During holiday family gatherings, Fels looked forward to Uncle Fred's visits. Sitting still and focused, Fels would listen as Fred shared stories of people being saved and crimes being solved. His uncle's detailed descriptions of how the crimes were solved and how justice was served enthralled Fels. He could see himself in a position where he would follow clues to solve crimes. He jotted down his many thoughts about it in his notebook.

By age 15, much to his father's displeasure, Fels was working in the sheriff's office in Wheatfield cleaning the office and the cells, and running errands for the sheriff. It was obviously not actual law enforcement work, but Fels felt as though he was directly immersed in the daily law enforcement activities. Fels still helped on the farm, but his younger siblings were now old enough to pick up much of the work. Fels did not like that he had to ignore many of his father's continual, unkind comments toward him.

With his ability to remain focused, however, Fels could observe every nuance of the activities of the sheriff and his single deputy. He kept notes as he learned how laws were enforced. He did his chores at the office well, but his ear was always tuned to the conversations and activities regarding the day-to-day law enforcement duties.

Fortunately for Fels, the sheriff liked the young man and felt himself something of a mentor to him. He was more than willing to answer Fels' numerous questions. The sheriff admired the inquisitiveness that Fels showed, and he appreciated the questions as they applied to someone who would pursue a law enforcement career. Fels was never a bother or nuisance to him.

Fels could see the logic, organization, and perseverance that was required of a law officer. After Uncle Fred had departed for Rochester following his visits, young Fels would search for "crimes" to solve and use his inquisitiveness and logic to bring the "crime" to resolution. His mother enjoyed seeing him actively engaging in the practice of his dreams. His father, on the other hand, could not stand to be around Fels any longer. He distanced himself from the boy, and Fels felt a bit of freedom like he had never known.

One day, Marie let Fels know that she had lost a pair of gloves. Fels put his crime-fighting and detective skills to use to solve the mystery of the stolen gloves. He questioned Marie in great detail about the gloves—their color, size, age—no detail was too small, he told her. He then focused on the last time Marie recalled wearing them. As the gloves were something Marie often wore, she was unsure of when she had not worn them. It puzzled Fels that she would not recall when she might not have worn them. But he knew that in detective work, one would not always have all the information at hand. It might take some time to uncover additional details about the situation.

Next, Fels asked her about her daily routine—when she would put the gloves on, when she would remove them. While Marie appreciated his interest, his questioning became tedious for her.

"Fels, I told you everything already. My gloves could be anywhere. I probably dropped them somewhere when I thought I placed them in my handbag. I just don't know." She was ready to give up. After all, she could pick up a new pair from her father's store.

"Now, that is a fresh development." Fels animatedly placed his hand on his chin and stared upward. "I think we need to retrace your steps throughout the day. Let's go! It'll be fun!"

"Oh, Fels." She lifted her eyes upward, but more pleadingly than thoughtfully.

Fels ignored her attempt to bring the investigation to an end. He grabbed her hand, and they headed out the door. "Let's walk to your father's store. We'll pay careful attention along the way."

"Fels, I would have had my gloves on until I arrived at the store. I would not have taken them off."

"C'mon, let's just walk." He squeezed her hand, and she looked sweetly into his eyes.

They made small talk as they walked. Fels wanted her to feel relaxed so that she might recall something. And, anyway, he enjoyed holding her hand.

A few minutes later, they turned a corner and proceeded about half-a-block until they neared Herriman's Grocery. Marie froze in her tracks.

"Fels, I stopped at Herriman's Thursday to get an apple for lunch. I looked through the bin of apples until I found one that looked good to me. Fels, I'm sure I took off my gloves to better feel the apple!"

"Let's go in and check with Mr. Herriman to see if anyone found a pair of gloves!"

They were both excited now, and the "crime" was solved when Mr. Herriman retrieved Marie's lost gloves from under his counter. Someone had found them next to the apple bin and brought them into the grocer.

"Mystery solved!" Fels stood tall and playfully boasted.

"Yes, you are quite the detective, Fels," she said with playful eyes. "But, really, thank you for finding my gloves." She put the gloves in her handbag and rejoined hands with Fels as they resumed their walk.

The comfort that Fels and Marie found in each other eventually turned to love. Marie's father had done all he could to end their relationship, however. He stopped short of forbidding her to see Fels. But he let Fels know in no uncertain terms that he had intended for his daughter to marry a "man of means."

CHAPTER 6

There was great interest as the Pan American Exposition opened in Buffalo in May of Fels' fifteenth year. There had been a heated competition between the cities of Buffalo and Niagara Falls over the location for the exposition. Buffalo won for two main reasons. First, Buffalo had a much larger population. With nearly 350,000 people, it was the eighth-largest city in the United States. Second, Buffalo had better railroad connections. The city was within a day's journey by rail for over 40 million people.

When the Spanish-American War broke out in 1898, the organizers put plans for the exposition on hold. As the war neared its end in July 1898, Congress pledged $500,000 for the exposition to be held at Buffalo. The advent of the alternating current power transmission system in the United States allowed designers to light the exposition in Buffalo using power generated 25 miles away at Niagara Falls. Upon completion of the construction, the grounds of the fair spread across 342 acres.

Fels was aware of the exposition, as there was talk in the law enforcement community of the difficulty there would be in managing the crowds. The sheriff was glad to be far away in the quiet Wheatfield farming community. When they found out that President McKinley would visit the exposition in September 1901, the law enforcement community started discussing the President's security concerns. In his own organized mind, Fels thought through the process of protecting the president under such circumstances. Maintaining some distance from the crowds that gathered would surely protect the President. And, certainly, his own security force would be large and ever on alert. He could imagine himself in such a position, keeping a watchful eye over the crowd as they pressed forward to see the President of the United States.

It was the morning of September 7 when the sheriff's office in Wheatfield received the news that President McKinley had been shot the previous day. While there had been discussions about security, it was surprising that someone had shot the president. The good news was that the president had survived the attempt on his life.

Fels was lost in understanding how this could happen. How could anyone do such a thing? Why would anyone do such a thing? None of it made sense to Fels, and it only further strengthened his resolve to pursue a profession in law enforcement.

Only two weeks later, September 14, President McKinley died from complications of his gunshot wound. Buffalo and the rest of the nation mourned at the news. Fels knew little about the politics of the country, but he did know that this was just so morally wrong. Yes, he would pursue a career in law enforcement.

At age 17, Fels was hired on as a full-time deputy with the sheriff in Wheatfield. He was no longer working on the farm with his family. His father was angry to the point that he refused to any longer speak with Fels. He felt Fels had betrayed his family. This situation did not sit well with Fels, but he had to pursue his own way in life. He had made the right decision for himself, and he was sure his father would one day forgive him.

Fels, however, still felt some responsibility for his family, especially for his mother. He gave a portion of his earnings to the family. That, of course, did nothing to appease his father. In fact, his father refused to take the money from Fels. Despite his father's rejection of Fels and his support for the family, Fels assured that his mother received the money. She and Fels continued to have a close relationship.

Fels' relationship with Marie grew ever stronger with each passing day. Her father was still not pleased with Fels' position in life, but he accepted Fels and admired the strength of his focus and direction. As he came to know Fels over time, he saw the moral character in the young man ... despite his continued concern with Fels' position in life.

Fels remained focused on his job as deputy, learning all that he could about the law and, perhaps just as importantly, about people. From the sheriff, Fels learned to understand what someone was not saying, or what they may be hiding. The sheriff taught him to watch a suspect's eyes and hands and notice generally how they carried their body. Fels quickly mastered the process of questioning a suspect or a witness. He developed the skill of asking the same question in different ways in order to validate a suspect's answers or catch them in a lie. Fels was also learning how to communicate with conviction while avoiding conflict. He was rapidly maturing in both a personal and professional manner.

After about two years with the Wheatfield sheriff, Fels obtained a job as a patrolman with the Tonawanda Police Department. The sheriff had provided a glowing recommendation for Fels. Fels expressed his gratitude to the sheriff for his confidence and all that he had taught him. The two left on the best of terms as Fels prepared for his move.

As a young recruit in Tonawanda, Fels was required to serve in the Traffic Control Unit. This duty involved monitoring the trolley cars, horse-drawn carts, and pedestrians in the more populated areas of town. It did not involve the crime fighting notion that Fels had in his mind concerning police work, but it sharpened his awareness of activities around him. The busy streets were chaotic, and it was the duty of the traffic patrol to keep order and safety. His head was constantly swiveling to maintain a keen awareness of his surroundings.

Carriage drivers and trolley passengers targeted their bitter comments toward the traffic patrol officer, and Fels was learning words he had never before heard spoken. In his usual manner, Fels took every moment as an opportunity to learn about people and to grow in his peaceful manner of dealing with problems.

Every new experience strengthened Fels. He developed the ability to remain calm in emotional situations that varied from frantic to impassioned to hysterical. As he expressed it, "Never let 'em see you sweat." He kept calm and eventually calmed others in such circumstances. Once the situation was under control, Fels would establish his authority and defuse the action.

It wasn't long before Fels moved to a neighborhood street patrol position where he learned about different ethnic and cultural values. He developed a rapport with the citizenry and soon became a respected figure in the neighborhood. It was a difficult position to achieve as the intercity police had a reputation through political control as being corrupt. Fels ignored the politics of the system and maintained control and peace in the diverse neighborhood.

His superiors noticed his abilities and moved him to various neighborhoods after evaluating his results. Fels

saw his movements to new neighborhoods as more opportunity to learn. He came to understand a wider diver-
sity of people, and the moves allowed him to study a
greater number of crimes and criminal types.

Fels eventually settled in at the 5th Precinct under
the guidance of Captain Orville Bruckhart. The two men
got along quite well with their mutual respect for the law
and their ability to see each person as the individual that
they were. They were both men who preferred their daily
activities to be well-organized. To both of them, the spirit
of the law was often more important than the letter of
the law. Both were excellent communicators.

The security Fels felt in his position, and his growing
confidence as a man, provided Fels the courage to ask
Marie to marry him. In June 1906, they became Mr. and
Mrs. Felsen Krieger. By this time, Marie's father had
come to accept Fels without hesitation about his role in
law enforcement. Fels could not have been happier.

A year later, Marie and Fels were expecting their first
child. Fels' father was still not speaking to his son, but
his mother supported Fels and Marie. Marie's father was
pleased that he would have his first grandchild. He had
warmed to Fels, and he treated him just as he would if
Fels were his own son.

Unfortunately, Marie miscarried. The family was
deeply saddened, but everyone encouraged the young
couple to keep trying to have children. Marie was very
grieved for a couple of months, but with plenty of love
and support, she recovered.

A year later, in 1908, their son Ludwig, named after
Fels' father, was born, and the year after that, their
daughter Frieda was born. Frieda was named after
Marie's mother, a decision that thrilled Marie's father.
The young couple were settling into a good life.

The same year Frieda was born, Fels accepted an offer from the Buffalo Police Department. The job as a pa-

trol officer in the Buffalo force came with a pay increase, which would help with Fels' growing family. As with his first move from sheriff deputy, Fels was highly recommended for the position in Buffalo. Within two years, the maturing police officer was promoted to the position of detective.

Fels began his new role as a detective with his usual spirit and attention to detail. Within the first year, however, his enthusiasm was extinguished. He discovered that corruption within the Buffalo Police Department was deep and wide. When Fels investigated a mob affiliated robbery ring, many men in the force refused to help him. He received warnings and threats not to continue with his investigation. There were definite ties between the mob and the politicians which, unfortunately, reached into the police department.

Fels' character would not let him do anything but the right thing. He pursued the investigation virtually alone. He broke up the ring and arrested not only some lower level gang members, but two mid-level mobsters. As a gateway between Canada and the United States, Buffalo was a key city for the Mafia in America. Fels had stirred a hornet's nest.

The existence of the Mafia in Western New York became apparent with the April 1903 discovery of a murdered Buffalo man within a barrel on a New York City sidewalk. Buffalo's "Little Italy" was located in what remained of the Erie Canal district on Buffalo's waterfront. Here the mob was fully operational, controlling the gambling and vice enjoyed by the longshoremen and sailors.

The first real boss of Buffalo's Mafia was Giuseppe "Don Pietro" DiCarlo. He was supported by his top lieutenant, Benedetto Angelo "Buffalo Bill" Palmeri. DiCarlo was born in Sicily in 1873. He and his family relocated from New York to Buffalo in 1908. DiCarlo was an associate of Manhattan-based Mafia boss of bosses Giuseppe Morello before his move.

DiCarlo built up powerful connections with other Italians around the country. Fellow countrymen sought him out for help, and he became the "big boss" of Buffalo. DiCarlo came up with a plan to organize crime, so there was more peace among the mob and more money for all to make. His plan succeeded, and as a result, he became the Buffalo boss. Under his leadership, DiCarlo took over the Italian district and the labor rackets on the docks. He owned the Buffalo Italian Importing Co., using it as a front for moving mob money.

Palmeri moved from New York City to Buffalo to become an important lieutenant in the DiCarlo regime. Two years later, Palmeri married into the DiCarlo family and moved into the DiCarlo household. Later, Palmeri moved his family to Niagara Falls, where he opened a cigar store, which served as a front for gambling rackets in association with the DiCarlo organization.

The Buffalo Mafia was well-organized and well-protected, both from within and without. The Mafia-controlled Black Hand was a mysterious extortion racket in which the victim received a letter demanding money or a threat of violence would result. It was often signed with the picture of a black hand. Occasionally, criminals used violence against law enforcement officials who battled Black Hand schemes. Victims of assassinations linked to Black Hand included at least two police officials. This was of special concern to Fels.

The mob's organization made it difficult to get through the lower layers to the upper levels of mob bosses and their lieutenants. Fels' arrests were at the highest levels ever achieved by the local law enforcement. He had gotten too close.

Threats grew stronger toward Fels following the arrests. With concern for his family, Fels resigned from the

Buffalo Police Department at the end of 1913. It was a tough decision for Fels to make. He was doing exactly what he was trained to do and exactly what the right thing was to do, but the corruption existed in such high places that Fels had to leave.

While Tonawanda was just north of Buffalo, it had a much better reputation than Buffalo. There had been some political corruption many years previously, but it had been quickly rooted out and cleaned up well before Fels had joined the department. The Tonawanda Police Department was very pleased to welcome Fels back, and they brought him onto the force in his current position as a detective.

Fels was assigned to 5th Precinct, where he had previously worked under Captain Bruckhart. Of course, Captain Bruckhart was now Chief of Police Bruckhart. Both men were glad to have their paths cross once again. The two men met in the chief's office on the day of Fels' return, where they talked a little about police work, but spent more time catching up on their personal lives.

"Say, Fels, is it true you own one of those motorized cycles?"

"Yep, I purchased it just over a year ago. Of course, Marie has never been happy with it. She refers to it as my 'foul motor bicycle.'" The two men laughed. "But I have to tell you, Chief, it's a fine way to get about. It's much faster than a bicycle, and easier to control than a horse!" They laughed again.

"I think you'll get along well with Captain Flynn here at the 5th. Dennis is one of the good ones. He's respected by all the men. He'll support you in every way. But he is a bit of a stickler for paperwork."

The discussion eventually turned more serious as Chief Bruckhart asked, "What about these threats from the mob, Fels? Do we need to put some men outside your home?"

Fels leaned back in his chair. "Oh, I don't think so, Chief. Look, there's a lot of corruption within the Buffalo force. I didn't imagine it was as bad as it was, but I do believe it was confined within their system. Now that they no longer have me around, I think it'll all be forgotten. They got what they wanted by pushing me out."

"What concerns me are the ties to the mob."

Fels interrupted, "Again, they wanted me out of there, and I'm out. I don't foresee any problems."

"I'd feel better with a man outside your home."

"Well, just have an extra patrol go by once in a while, if it'll make you feel better. I really don't think we need to take an officer out of duty to sit at my house."

"Okay, Fels, we'll go with your instincts."

Fels awoke with a start. *How could I have been so blind!? I should have known they would try something.*

CHAPTER 7

Fels' body was healing with each passing day, but he grew increasingly despondent over the loss of his family. His heart, worse than being crushed, had become hardened as stone. Nothing mattered to him, not even himself.

His understanding of any feeling was lost. He was cut off, isolated, from the world he had once known and enjoyed. The love and joy of his life were taken the night of the explosion. What else was there to live for? His strongest, and to him clearest, thought was that if he had his service revolver, he could join his family.

Nothing around him offered an alternative. Every voice, every sound, was as a distant echo. It was as though he was no longer taking part in life; it moved along without him. He was simply an outside observer of those things in which he could not take part. He might as well be dead.

Fels' physical healing encouraged Dr. Bellamy, and he let Fels know how well he was progressing. Fels seemed not to care, and Dr. Bellamy easily recognized it. He had seen this in patients who had experienced a devastating loss such as Fels had. He knew he had to reach Fels before he slipped farther away.

"Fels, you know how pleased I am with your physical recovery. I'll be able to release you soon, but you must put in the work to get yourself back in good physical condition for your police work. I have some thoughts on that for you." He felt that if he could push Fels into physical activity, it would help cure his depression.

Dr. Bellamy paused as Fels turned his face directly to the doctor. He saw the doctor as if looking through a veil. Fels stared blankly and spoke through the veil, "Police work? That's the farthest thing from my mind." He turned his face away from the doctor.

"Look, Fels, I know you're hurting, but you have plenty of people who care for you."

"Care for me?! I have nothing! I am nothing! I've lost everything I care about! I have nothing!"

"Fels, ..."

"Go away!!"

The doctor knew not to push Fels any further at this point. "I'll be back later. Right now, I'll have a nurse give you something to help you calm down."

Fels did not reply as the doctor left. Fels could not even bring himself to cry over his situation. He found himself lost and saw no way out. A nurse arrived shortly thereafter and gave Fels an injection. He was soon fast asleep. Sleep was his only source of occasional peace.

But even the peace of sleep did not last long for Fels. His nights were now filled with horrific images. No matter the details of the nightmares, they were always filled with the explosion, the all-encompassing inferno, and the screams of his wife and children. Fels would find himself engulfed in the flames, unable to reach his family. He felt their horror and pain night after night, awakening each morning in a sweat-soaked bed.

He was eating little, and he took little care to provide for the healing of his injuries. The nurses had trouble coaxing him out of bed to make even the shortest of walks. When he did walk, he plodded along with little awareness of his surroundings.

Fels remained wrapped in his veil, where he used his waking hours to plot revenge against the murderer of his family. He would pursue justice for his family. Whether that justice was in a court of law or at Fels' own hands didn't matter to him. One way or another, justice would be served for his family. It was the only pretext that gave him the slightest bit of will to live.

Worried about Fels' state of mind, Dr. Bellamy brought in a psychologist to talk with Fels. Fels, of course, was reluctant at first, but after a few days, he found it useful, although not necessarily helpful, to talk with the psychologist. He could see that maybe, with a little more focus, he could get out of the hospital and pursue his revenge.

The hospital chaplain also visited Fels and said some of the same things as the psychologist, only with a religious twist. Both men tried to help Fels see a need for purpose. They spoke to him about family and friends and work.

Fels remained standoffish to all of their appeals. Any talk of his family drove Fels to anger. He was angry with the doctors, he was angry with the nurses, he was angry with himself, and most of all, he was angry with whoever had done this to him. His anger was driving him to discover a purpose. Yes, he would use his new purpose to find the energy he needed to heal. He must heal in order to hunt down the butcher who had slaughtered his family.

The doctors and chaplain eventually convinced Fels to ask himself what Marie would want. If they wanted him to go there, then Fels would. The conversation had been difficult for Fels, but the doctors saw a change in him. He explained he understood the need for purpose, and he was now seeing that. Fels seemed to have sparked a renewed interest in living. The doctors were hopeful for Fels.

But the doctors didn't know that Fels' new sense of purpose was one of vengeance. He focused his heart of stone on finding the murderer and ensuring that justice was meted out. Justice? The courts would be too lenient in Fels' mind. Justice would belong to Fels, and to him alone. What would Marie want? She would want to be alive and at home with Fels and their children. But she had been robbed of that—he had been robbed of that. Whoever brought this upon them would pay.

Fels did not even realize he had hit the bottom. His sight of hope and love had vanished. The love he had once shared with his family had vanished from his mind. He had forgotten how he and Marie had fallen to their knees and prayed when they had lost their first child. He had forgotten how to find peace with God in difficult times. The many times God had given them hope in the midst of trouble in their lives together had slipped from his mind. God was always by his side, but Fels had stopped turning to him. Fels was so very lost.

For Fels, his new purpose opened a small tear in his veiled existence. He did not recognize that such a purpose would not offer him the freedom he thought he might get in this pursuit. That small bit of purpose, as misguided as it was, might provide a way out for Fels, however.

Fels continued going through the motions with the doctor and the nurses. They were all very encouraging about his physical recovery. While they did not see a full sense of an emotional recovery, they all felt that Fels seemed to be making some progress. He was working harder at his recovery, which they took to mean he was working through his depression.

But Fels was fooling all of them. He was set on vengeance—that was his real purpose. He had to get stronger so he could find the killer of his family. The police had made no progress. He was completely dissatisfied with the meager efforts of law enforcement. Why hadn't they made an arrest yet? How could they not have a suspect? Was the lack of progress related to his arrests while at the Buffalo PD? Was the Mafia involved?! In his mind, it was up to him, and him alone, to take care of the matter. And he would regain his physical abilities to do just that.

At the end of the week, Dr. Bellamy stopped to see Fels in the morning. "Fels, I think we're going to be releasing you tomorrow. How do you feel about that?" He wanted to give Fels something hopeful to look forward to.

Fels lifted himself up in the bed, displaying the strength he had gained and the desire he feigned to move on. "I'm ready to get out of here." He felt he should smile, but he could not even bring himself to do that. He tried to hide this inability by appearing tired. "I'm sure I'll sleep much better away from this place."

"Well, good. Tomorrow it is. Do you have somewhere to stay? Perhaps a friend or relative?"

Fels did not want to be around anyone else, and he certainly would not stay with his parents. "Chief Bruckhart was kind enough to arrange a room for me. I think that will do just fine for now."

Fels felt it would be beneficial to express more gratitude for the hospital's efforts on his behalf. He extended his hand to the doctor, and they politely shook hands. "Thanks for everything, doc. I know I was not the best patient for some time there."

"In a couple of weeks, we'll be able to get that cast off, too." Dr. Bellamy smiled, and Fels forced a smile in return. It felt completely awkward.

The doctor continued going over some details of the current state of Fels' injuries. Fels paid little attention as his thoughts turned to finding the killer. In his typically organized mind, Fels had already started outlining the process. He was hopeful he could get his hands on the files of everything that the police had done to date. That would serve as his starting point.

"... So, I've written the address and the name of the gymnast at Turners I would like you to see."

Fels shook his head. "I'm sorry. My mind must have wandered off for a moment. You were saying?"

"I was saying that I have made arrangements for you to work on your physical strengthening at the Turner Society. I've referred several severely injured patients to the Turners for recovery under a rehabilitation plan they will provide for your specific needs. Fels, you must put in the hard work to recover so that you can resume your duties with the police department." What began as a trial to see if the Turners could help patients like Fels had become a plan the doctor was now willing to openly promote.

"I understand."

"As I was saying, here is the address for Turners, and this is the individual I want you to see, George Wagner."

Fels took the piece of paper from Dr. Bellamy. "Of course."

"Fels, you are also going to need support to recover from the loss of your family. This may be more difficult than your physical recovery. I suggest you get in touch with the psychologist you met here. Or, if you would prefer, talk to the pastor at your church." He held out his hand to Fels and grasped Fels' hand firmly in both of his own hands. "Fels, don't try to go this alone."

Sorry, but it is up to me alone! The individual re-sponsible for this devastation will pay! I will see to it! Fels felt himself losing control and quickly tried to contain himself. He needed to respond without hesitation. "Yes, never alone. Thanks, doc."

The doctor released his hold on Fels' hand, noting that his pulse had increased. He supposed his patient was eager to get out of the hospital and continue his recovery. Dr. Bellamy smiled to himself as he left the room.

Later that afternoon, a young man arrived to assist Fels with his mobility exercises. He was attired more like a doctor than a nurse. He was dressed in a white coat with a surgeon's cap on his head. He did have a stethoscope like those that the nurses sometimes had with them.

Fels thought he was doing fine on his own, but he accepted the young man's help. The nurses had helped him out of bed a few times, but this man had greater strength to assist Fels in and out of bed.

"Mr. Krieger, you must be eager to be getting out of the hospital." The young man was cheerful, but not overly so. He seemed to know just the right tone to take with Fels. He continued, "You know, it's great to have a renewed sense of purpose. What changed for you?"

It sounded like a simple matter-of-fact question the way the young man spoke the words. However, Fels was stunned by what he perceived as a very pointed question. What would this young man know about his purpose? "What do you mean, 'What changed?'"

"Oh, I know how you've been struggling with your emotional recovery. I would imagine it was a little like drowning—feeling helpless and hopeless, unable to even breathe. So, what changed for you?" Again, the young man was very matter-of-fact with his question. He seemed to speak as if he and Fels knew one another.

Fels' near-drowning in the pond when he was only ten years old flashed through his mind. Fels thought he should be angry with the young man's insolence, but he felt something different. He couldn't bring himself to admit that he felt a sense of caring coming from the young man. Fels was puzzled.

"I needed something to bring me back to the surface. Yes, I was drowning. I guess that's a good way to look at it."

"Well, you know, there are positive and negative purposes, good and bad purposes." The young man helped Fels to his feet from the hospital bed.

Fels thought the young man spoke with more wisdom than his age should allow.

"Both can be effective, but only one can have a worthy outcome." He paused and looked deeply into Fels' eyes. "Perhaps you should think about your purpose. Examine your life and understand your bigger purpose. You know, that bigger purpose that God has for you."

Fels' heart, however, was still very hardened. That word "purpose" brought his mind directly to his self-realized purpose: to bring vengeance upon the killer of his family. Still, there was something tugging at him that he could not put his finger on.

The two were now walking together down the hallway. Supported by the young man, Fels could feel his obvious strength. He almost made Fels feel weightless. But there was another form of strength that Fels could feel flowing from the young man. *What is this? Did he talk to the chaplain? No, I didn't even express my true feelings to him. Does he know my desire for revenge, or is he just probing?*

As if they were having a conversation, the young man said, "No one has told me anything about your plans. I'm just saying don't get lost. Stay focused on what's right and good." The young man turned his face to Fels and smiled. Fels stared back blankly.

They walked some more before returning to Fels' room. Settled back in bed, Fels thanked the young man for his help.

"You're welcome." As the young man left the room, he turned back toward Fels and said, "I suppose we may meet again. You will get well, and you will come to find the peace and hope you have lost. As the Psalmist wrote, 'The Lord is close to the brokenhearted and saves those who are crushed in spirit.'"

Fels sat in bed, stunned and perplexed by the things the young man had said. He tried to shut out those things and focus on his plan for vengeance. What he failed to see was the smallest crack in his plan that was opened by God.

CHAPTER 8

Chief Bruckhart had arranged an apartment for Fels in Tonawanda close to the local Turnverein, or Turner Society, and near to the hospital. The accommodations featured a small and simple layout, making it easy for Fels to get around in and care for. The front door opened into a sparsely furnished parlor that extended the width of the apartment. At the rear to the left was the single bedroom with a bed and a chest of drawers. At the rear to the right was the small kitchen equipped with dishes and pots and pans. It contained a window providing some outdoor light that reached into the living room. There was another window in the bedroom. Wedged in between next to the bedroom was a small bathroom.

For even more convenience, the apartment was heated using steam heating. Fels would not need to gather firewood for a fireplace. In addition, the kitchen was equipped with a gas stove. Chief Bruckhart had thought of every convenience in helping Fels live comfortably while he recovered. He had also seen to it that the kitchen was stocked with some basic necessities to get Fels started. Sitting on a small kitchen table were a jar filled with cookies and an apple pie that the chief's wife had made.

Fels had very few belongings, since he had lost everything in the fire. The chief brought a few things while Fels was in the hospital. He was kind enough to pick up some clothing for Fels prior to his release. Fels was grateful for the kindness of Chief Bruckhart. Now, Fels could move forward if he could count on the chief to provide information to find the killer.

Fels had a place to lay his head. He had all the basic essentials. He needed little more. While he had once dressed well, mostly at Marie's insistence, he now gave no thought to his attire. He only needed the most basic clothing. Food was not that important to him. With little appetite, he would just grab something whenever he felt the need. What he needed was paper and pencils to work on his case. That was his first priority. After he had the supplies he needed to work on his case, he would go to Turners and continue his physical recovery. He didn't think a psychologist or pastor was necessary.

Two days after settling in to his new location, Fels arrived at the Turner Society. The Turners were not organized to support a rehabilitation program as such, but their promotion of physical fitness fit neatly into such an endeavor. After all, their motto said it all, "Strong Mind in a Strong Body."

When the Turners had arrived in American in 1848, a Turnverein was a gymnastics club that promoted German culture and physical fitness. In the mid-1800s, the Turners lobbied school boards in America to include Physical Education in the public school curriculum. They were successful with the first school program in 1855.

A Turnverein served as a political and social center for new immigrants in the early days. They acted as a social club hosting social events, parades, and musical events. But at their core, they promoted physical fitness and exercise through their gymnastics program.

Turners opposed all forms of oppression, and as champions of equal rights, they firmly opposed slavery. Because of founder Vater Jahn's principals of liberty and equality, they were the first to volunteer for the Union Army at the beginning of the Civil War; in fact, two-thirds of the Turners in America signed up. Their military training and discipline helped provide leadership for the Army. Turners stood guard at President Abraham Lincoln's Inauguration, and they made up the Honor Guard at his funeral.

Recent anti-German propaganda made things difficult for many Germans in America. Although still a German club, they changed the official club language to English in order to reassure their fellow countrymen that they were Americans. With the large German population in Western New York, the organization was generally well-accepted.

Fels' recovery at the club began at a slow pace. He wasn't ready to move forward after losing his family, and only sought physical rehabilitation so he could prepare for revenge. His heart was hardened and his body was weak.

George Wagner, a talented gymnast, was given charge of Fels. His body was well-toned with a muscular chest and arms, typical of a gymnast. His hair was neatly trimmed, and he sported a well-groomed handlebar mustache. He was a friendly and optimistic young man who always greeted Fels with a cheerful, encouraging word. Dr. Bellamy had worked with George to rehabilitate other patients in the past. Everyone of them made great gains working with George.

Fels did not care for the daily cheerful word and the manner in which George encouraged Fels to clear his mind and direct his thoughts. All Fels wanted to do was regain his strength so he could find his family's killer. It was a single purpose that Fels felt would help him focus on getting strong. Fels would be ready to work only so he could pursue vengeance.

Fels pushed himself hard physically. With each bit of gain, George only pushed Fels further. Fels appreciated this aspect of the rehabilitation program. As weeks went by and Fels gained greater range of motion, George moved Fels into more strengthening exercises. Week after week, Fels saw the gains in his own flexibility and muscle tone.

George never abandoned Fels' mental well-being. He had been made aware of Fels' deep loss by Dr. Bellamy. He convinced Fels to begin a meditation exercise by telling Fels it would provide additional strength for his body to get his mind focused. It was somewhat true, but George's actual goal was to develop an improved attitude in Fels about his current situation and to help him see a future for himself.

On one particularly difficult morning, a young man who had noticed Fels' struggles with some simple warm-up stretching approached Fels. Fels was grumbling to himself when the young man appeared at Fels' side.

With a cheerful smile and a friendly openness, the man said, "Good morning, Mr. Krieger."

Fels scowled at the young man. "Tell me one good thing about it," Fels challenged.

"The sun's shining, and you're healing," was his quick, cheerful reply. He wore the attire that most of the gymnasts wore. His short-sleeved shirt exposed a well-toned torso and muscular arms. The young man was obviously physically fit. He was of medium height with tousled, wavy brown hair. He seemed familiar to Fels, but he could not quite place him.

The quick answer did not impress Fels, but he felt a sense of peace and joy in the young man. In an instant, his scowl was gone. Fels tried not to smile, but he couldn't help it.

"That's such a superficial answer that it's almost laughable. In fact, it is laughable," and Fels chuckled.

"Good. It made you laugh!"

"Okay, thanks for the laugh." A smile remained on Fels' face.

"You're welcome."

"How'd you know my name?"

"Oh, I assist here from time to time, so I'm familiar with the people the Turners work with in these rehabilitation programs."

Fels now recognized the direct approach of the young man from the hospital. "It's you! You were the one who worked with me in the hospital the day before I was released." It angered him that the young man had not exposed himself, almost as if he was trying to hide his identity.

"Sorry about that. I should have introduced myself. Yes, I was at the hospital with you."

Fels asked almost indignantly, "And you are?"

"Smith ... David Smith. I just thought I'd see how you're doing. George has had some concern about your state of mind, you know." He paused for a moment to see if Fels wanted to speak. Fels continued looking at David.

"Anyway, you seem to be coming along quite well with your rehab. Your attitude is an enormous part of the recovery process. I know George's meditation thing can be overwhelming, but just consider it a little time to spend in quiet prayer. Sometimes all you have to do is just be still and listen for God's voice to wash through you."

Fels lifted his eyes upward momentarily. "I see. My wife often told me to sit quietly and listen for God's voice. In my line of work, my mind is always cluttered with other things, I guess."

"I think your wife was a very astute woman in Godly matters."

Fels briefly considered berating the young man for mentioning his wife, but the feeling of her love washed the thought away.

"So, what about the purpose search? Any thoughts?"

"Oh, I still have a purpose. It keeps me focused on getting stronger each day. Everyone tells me how pleased they are with my progress, so I suppose it's serving me well."

Manifesting warmth and calmness, David challenged Fels, and Fels felt the care that was being delivered in the challenge. "No, Fels, remember your bigger purpose. What does God have planned for you? Have you talked with Him? Have you asked Him for guidance?"

Fels ignored the challenge about a bigger purpose. "I've been driven by the need to find my family's killer. That has kept me going and working hard in my rehabilitation. I need to find the person who did this and see that ... justice ... is served." As the words crossed his lips, Fels felt himself repulsed by the thought of revenge. He did not understand his feelings. He wondered why he was so confused by David's challenge.

"I know it can be confusing, but you have to come to terms with your true purpose, the purpose for which you were created. It is a purpose that will bring out the best of your gifts and talents. It is a purpose with which you can serve others." David paused. "Fels, you were on the right road, but this tragedy has gotten you lost."

Fels' head was swimming. It was all so confusing and yet so simple at the same time.

David could see that he had upset Fels more than he had intended. "Fels, take some deep breaths."

Fels breathed deeply and slowly exhaled several times as George had taught him. "I don't understand. Are you a pastor or something? The hospital chaplain was nice enough, but he just didn't make it so straight-forward as you do. Do you really believe in what you called a 'bigger purpose'?"

David placed a hand on Fels' shoulder. "Yes." He paused. "And so do you. You will see." Then David turned and disappeared through a nearby doorway.

Despite being stupefied, Fels called after him, "Thanks, David."

Over more weeks, George noticed a slight change in Fels' attitude. He no longer scorned George's cheerful welcome to start each session. Fels was on the right road to full recovery, and he could feel it himself.

At his apartment, Fels was taking better care of himself. His diet was beneficial for both his physical and mental well-being. And, best of all, Fels could now think of his family without breaking down. He, in fact, found himself talking to Marie as if she were actually present. It wasn't in an odd sort of way, but just a recognition of her impact on Fels' life. It became a comfort for Fels.

As fall approached, Fels had grown strong physically and emotionally. He had never been in better health and physical shape, not even during his days on the farm.

It was on a day when he was feeling at his peak that Fels visited the vacant lot where his house had once been. At the rear of the property stood the dilapidated old milk barn. It was at that moment that Fels remembered his motorcycle. He had not thought of it since the explosion.

Walking to the barn, he carefully made his way through some fallen timbers and found his motorcycle. He removed a tarp he had placed over it and found the motorcycle just as he had left it. The gas tank was filled, and Fels decided to try to start it. As he swung his leg over the seat, *Fels, I hope you are not going to ride that foul motor bicycle down to the tavern.*

He stopped with his leg resting on the seat and swiveled his head. "Who's there?" He placed his foot on the ground beside the motorcycle and turned around to scan the interior of the dilapidated barn. "I said, who's there?" There was nothing but silence.

Fels jumped off the motorcycle, ran outside the barn, and looked around. There was no one to be seen. *Did I hear that, or was it my imagination?* Fels was confused. *I heard that. It was just as if Marie was standing next to me.* "Marie, are you here?" he whispered into the air. No reply was to be heard. Fels felt it must be his mind playing tricks on him.

He stepped back into the barn and walked over to the motorcycle. After several minutes, he got the Harley-Davidson started. Fels savored the noise of the engine and the smell of the burning fuel. It was comforting to him. He revved the motor several times in preparation for riding the motorcycle back to his apartment. But once again, *Fels, I hope you are not going to ride that foul motor bicycle down to the tavern.* He turned off the motor and called out, "Who's there?! I'm tiring of this game! Show yourself!"

He ran out of the barn expecting to find someone, but once again, the area was empty. "Whoever you are, this is a very sick trick! I'm leaving, and I better not find you here again!" With that, Fels went into the barn, started the motorcycle, and drove away.

CHAPTER 9

Behind the apartment Fels occupied was a tool shed he had gained approval to use to store his motorcycle. While a bicycle was good exercise for him to make his way to Turners, the motorcycle would save him time. By late-September, Fels was cleared by the doctor, and his rehabilitation program at Turners could be discontinued. However, Fels wanted to retain the gains he had made in his physical condition and continued to complete a regular exercise program three or four days a week. He was enjoying the newfound strength and agility his body had developed.

But he now had to focus on the task foremost in his mind, finding his family's killer. While he was in a better place mentally, he still sought revenge for the deaths. He had convinced himself that it was not so much revenge as it was a need to see the law upheld and the killer brought to justice. It was his way of saying that he was not out for revenge—that he had changed—but deep inside, he had not yet healed and reconciled himself with God.

Fels informed his captain that he would not yet be returning to work. He had convinced the captain he needed additional time to resolve his physical health and his mental outlook. No one questioned Fels' time off and only encouraged him to take as much time as he needed. And that was exactly what he planned to do. He would take as much time as was needed to find the coward who had killed his family.

Fels had kept in touch with Captain Flynn on the progress of the case. He had worked for Flynn since his promotion four years ago. They had a professional working relationship, certainly not a personal or warm relationship. Fels was fine with this as a subordinate to Flynn, and he appreciated Flynn's professionalism. Fels had learned a good deal from Flynn over the past several years. Under Flynn's tutelage, Fels had honed his skills and was especially good at understanding and following his own instincts.

Fels' relationship with Chief Bruckhart was very different. Bruckhart was more like a father to Fels. He was encouraging and warm with all of his men. There was no doubt who was in charge and who had the last word, but Chief Bruckhart could be a friend, a pastor, or a teacher who would truly listen and offer advice, not directives. Although, Fels always found himself choosing the advice as if it were a directive to follow. But Chief Bruckhart helped Fels to make a good choice on his own. Fels thought there weren't many men like Chief Bruckhart.

Unfortunately, according to Captain Flynn, the trail had turned cold on the murder of Fels' family. The police were still unsure as to the motive. They had looked into many of the men Fels had arrested, but no one appeared to be a suspect. And, so far, no one had heard any rumors on the streets.

Fels, however, had his own suspicions and theory. Fels had never fallen into the corruption trap that existed in the Buffalo Police Department. He recalled how he had also ruffled a few feathers when he broke up a local

gang of thieves with direct ties to the mob. Unfortunately, all the men were released through corrupt connections within the Buffalo Police Department. As a result, none of the men were on the list of suspects in Fels'
case—they were now on Fels' list, however.

Fels, and of course all of Tonawanda and Buffalo law
enforcement, knew the explosion had not been a mob
hit. While they could be cold-blooded killers in their
business dealings, the mob held family in the highest esteem. Wives and children were off-limits. This was a rule
that would not be broken without extreme consequences
for the guilty. So, Fels was sure this had not been a mob
action.

Some had suggested the Black Hand, but Fels had received no letter, and that was the standard mode of operation for the Black Hand. The *modus operandi* of the
Black Hand involved extortion. There was no extortion
demand received. There was simply nothing about the
events involving Fels' family that would lead to any suspicion of the Black Hand.

On occasion, criminals had used violence against law
enforcement officials who battled Black Hand schemes.
Victims of assassinations linked to Black Hand included
at least two police officials. But, in all cases, the victims
had first received a letter with specific demands. No, Fels
easily eliminated the Black Hand as a suspect.

While he had his own list of suspects, Fels felt that
the explosion, the very intensity of such an action, just
made no sense. It didn't add up for him now, but he was
determined to discover the truth of the event.

Fels began making inquiries on the streets. After
some initial investigation, Fels was left with five names
on his list. Knowing the neighborhood in which the men
had been arrested, Fels began making inquiries. Fels discovered that only one name on the list still lived in the
neighborhood. Fels located his family, but the individual

had joined the U.S. Army several months ago and was stationed at a new camp in Gettysburg, Pennsylvania, at the time of the explosion. The family gave Fels the names of some of the man's acquaintances, and two of those names were on Fels' list.

Fels located the families of the two men in Niagara Falls. One man had been killed in a robbery gone bad only weeks after Fels had arrested him. The other man had fled the area after they released him, and he had not been heard from since. Further investigative work proved this story to be true. As best as Fels could determine, the man had fled to Kansas City and had never returned.

Two names remained. Fels suspected both men may also be in the Niagara Falls area. After some follow-up, Fels discovered that one of the men, John Mosher, had been in the hospital at the time of the explosion. He could not uncover any information about the other man, Paul Sporco.

After two more days of legwork, Fels located John Mosher. With nothing else to go on, Fels decided to question Mosher about the whereabouts of Paul Sporco. Fels waited outside the Dobbie Foundry and Machine Company where Mosher worked on Portage Road and followed Mosher for several blocks until he entered a tavern. Fels decided not to follow him into the tavern, and instead watched from outside until Mosher left the establishment.

He followed Mosher for two blocks until he came to an area of several abandoned buildings. It was there that Fels approached Mosher. At first, he told Fels he did not know the other man. Fels' keen instincts told him that Mosher was lying. Mosher became skittish, and Fels feared he would run. So, Fels collared the man and swept him into one of the abandoned buildings, cautiously checking to be sure no one was watching.

Fels took Mosher into a back room, where he forced him to sit in a wooden chair. He then tied Mosher securely to the chair with cord from an electric lamp. Mosher had struggled against Fels, but the man put up little fight as he was weak and frightened.

As Fels finished tightening the cords on Mosher's hands, Mosher pleaded, "Look, I don't know what's going on. What do you want? I don't have any money! Check my pockets! Please, don't do this!"

"Sit quietly, Mr. Mosher. Answer my questions, and you can be on your way home."

"What questions? What do you want? How do you know my name?"

Fels leaned forward into Mosher's face. "I want answers. Let's start with a simple question, shall we? This should be easy, since I've already asked it. Do you know Paul Sporco?"

"I already told you. I don't know that name!"

Fels was inches away from Mosher's face. "You're lying to me! I won't put up with it! Tell me the truth!"

Mosher sobbed. "I am."

"How about this? How many beers did you have at the tavern?"

"What?"

Once again face-to-face, Fels screamed, "How many beers did you drink!"

"F-f-four. I had four glasses."

Fels smiled. "Well, look how easy that was. I was watching you. Yes, you did have four glasses of beer. Now, that was not so hard, was it?"

"How do you know Paul Sporco?!"

Mosher sobbed again. "I don't know him."

Fels stood, stiff with anger. He leaned back and delivered a blow to Mosher's side. The chair nearly tipped over from the blow, but Fels kept Mosher from falling to the dirty floor. Fels glared at Mosher, who was bent over in the chair and moaning.

Fels was now on the verge of rage. He had used constraint until his anger got the best of him, and he struck Mosher. It was as if the floodgates had been opened, and Fels pummeled the man's body with three more quick blows with the strength he had gained at Turners.

Mosher's head was down as he cried. Fels grabbed Mosher's hair and lifted his head. He screamed at Mosher. "Tell me about Paul Sporco!"

"I—I—I ...."

Fels hit Mosher squarely in the stomach, causing him to retch. The smell of beer filled the area.

Fels was breathing heavily. "I can do this all night! Can you?!"

"No. Stop. Please. Stop."

Fels lifted Mosher's head again, looked into his eyes, and lifted his fist above his head, preparing for another blow.

"I know Sporco! I know him!"

Fels let go of Mosher's hair. He had anticipated Mosher would easily give up the information he was after, but the man took more punishment than Fels had expected.

Mosher gave up. He could not take anymore punishment and admitted to knowing the other man. Mosher cried out to Fels of his fear of Paul Sporco. Mosher told Fels that the man threatened to kill him if he spoke to anyone, but especially to the law. With his training and experience, Fels was sure that Mosher honestly feared for his life.

Paul Sporco was the last name left on Fels' list of suspects. Fels felt more convinced than ever that he had pinpointed his prime suspect. Sporco was the killer. Mosher said that Sporco had threatened to kill his entire family by blowing up his house if he said anything! This had to be his man.

Mosher gave Fels everything he knew about the whereabouts of Sporco. He lived in Niagara Falls but hadn't seen him since the explosion at Fels' home. Fels talked about a timeline of events with Mosher, but he had not mentioned that the explosion had killed his family. Mosher claimed to have been in the hospital on the date of the explosion. Fels knew that to be true.

Once Mosher began talking, he spilled his guts to Fels. Sporco, like Mosher, was trying to win his way into the mob. His apprehension in a robbery broken up by a particular Buffalo police detective had embittered Sporco. He felt the arrest by the cop made him look bad in his attempt to gain entry into the mob.

Sporco planned to showcase his explosive expertise to grab the mob's attention. He would kill the cop who had arrested him. He would do it in a big way, making his name known to the mob. Mosher didn't quite understand since the police had released them, but he told Fels that Sporco was a very vengeful person with a short temper.

Mosher told Fels he had heard that it all backfired on Sporco because he had killed the cop's family. According to Mosher, the mob would never give a thought to Sporco because of that. He knew Sporco was trying to lay low, but he did not know where he lived. He told Fels that Sporco had worked at the Carborundum Company, but he didn't know if he was still there. No further details were provided by Mosher. He begged Fels not to reveal that he had provided this information. He greatly feared for his life.

Fels assured Mosher he would not reveal the source of his information to anyone. Fels made it clear to Mosher that if he talked to Sporco or anyone else about their conversation, he would face unpleasant consequences. Fels, of course, had not used his real name, or the fact that he was a detective with the Tonawanda Police. He released Mosher, who ran out the door of the building, holding his side. Fels then sat down in the chair that he had tied Mosher to.

Fels was not comfortable with what he had done. He had never abused a suspect under interrogation. Sure, he had used harsh words and threats with suspects, but he had gone beyond that with Mosher. He was cautious to keep all of his blows to the man's body and not his face. While Fels was sure Mosher was hurting, there was no physical evidence to reveal the mistreatment he had inflicted. It should have given him a sense of satisfaction to find the name of his suspect, for he was one step closer to achieving vengeance. A persistent nagging haunted his thoughts, however. It wasn't about the suspect, but rather it was about his own lack of self-control. He had stepped over a line that he had sworn he never would.

Fels sat still in the chair in the empty building with his head lowered. *Yeah, but I got the information I needed. I can bring in my family's killer now.* But he wasn't feeling the satisfaction he had expected to feel.

Fels, it is not like you. I'm sorry you felt you had to act like this, but know that we are fine. You will be fine, too.

Upon hearing the voice, Fels looked up, expecting to see Marie's gentle face. He scanned the area to see who had spoken to him. But he was alone in the wooden chair. *Surely, I must have imagined that. Get control, Fels.* He scanned the vacant structure again. *It must be my conscience.* "But, Marie, if that is you, I'm sorry."

Fels again lowered his head into his hands. A sense of shame washed over him. He was trying to hide from the actions he had just taken. He sobbed a bit, and then he sighed and lifted his head. There was additional work that needed to be done.

CHAPTER 10

Just days after Fels had coerced the information from John Mosher, a well-dressed and well-mannered man approached Fels just outside the entrance of Turners after his exercise program. Fels was standing still, filling his lungs with the cool, fresh air, and he did not notice the man until he spoke to Fels.

"Excuse me, Detective Krieger?" The man smiled and offered a polite handshake to Fels.

Quickly becoming alert to the man's presence, Fels couldn't help but notice his well-starched cuffs and shirt collar. His suit was of obvious top quality, and his shoes appeared to have just been polished. Fels showed no emotion as he firmly shook the gentleman's hand.

"Yes," Fels said, and offered nothing more. Looking him straight in the eyes, he waited for the man to introduce himself.

"Hello. I'm Field Agent Myron Blackmon of the Bureau of Investigation with the Justice Department. I apologize for inserting myself into your day unannounced. I was hoping we could speak. Perhaps over a cup of coffee?"

"Agent Blackmon. Yes, we met while I was on the Buffalo force. I recall you were involved in an investigation of the Italian mob, the Mafia."

Fels remembered the agent's name from his time with the Buffalo Police Department, but he never really got to know the man. At the time of their acquaintance, Fels had already lost support of most of the police force because of his investigation into the Mafia's activities. He had no interest in bringing someone else into the mix —someone whom he did not know, and therefore, could not assume to trust. His manner of dress alone, as Fels now recalled, brought a suspicion to Fels. After all, how many law enforcement officers dressed as well as he did? He wondered if the BOI agent was being paid off by the mob, like others in Buffalo. So, he avoided any cooperation with the agent until he could determine his motives. As the case was dismissed, Fels dismissed any engagement with the agent.

"Yes, that's correct. And I remember you were heavily involved, but you were not getting much appreciation from the other officers. They sent me in to dig deeper, but as I recall, you were suspicious of a newcomer to the case."

"It was nothing personal. I just didn't feel there was anyone I could trust at that point."

Agent Blackmon motioned ahead with his left hand and a polite smile. "Perhaps we could sit down at the coffee shop down the street."

"Of course." Fels wanted to find out what he could about a federal agent showing a sudden interest in his activities and, perhaps, in the death of his family. Maybe he was legitimate and Fels could probe him for information.

The two men walked side by side without exchanging further words and entered the coffee shop. They both eyed a booth near the rear of the shop. Nodding to a waitress, the two men took seats at the booth and ordered coffee. Agent Blackmon spoke first, picking up where their conversation had left off outside of Turners.

"I've been investigating the Mafia in Western New York for several years. The Bureau has had some success in Rochester, but the Buffalo organization has been very elusive. My expertise is in business and banking. We know they're using the Buffalo Italian Importing business to cover their tracks, but we've not been able to infiltrate the business. The Bureau hoped I could look through their accounting records and uncover any illegal activities; however, we have never been able to get our hands on anything other than their 'cooked' books."

"So, why are you telling this to me?" Fels was short with the agent. What did he care about the agent's inability to get his hands on the Mafia's accounts? He had more pressing issues to deal with, and an expert in business and banking was not going to help him bring in his family's killer.

"Detective Krieger, I followed your investigation at the Buffalo PD and the ultimate arrests with some detail. You came as close as anyone, even closer than the BOI, to cracking into the upper levels of the organization." He paused here. His calm command of the conversation changed.

"Detective, please let me stop here and offer my condolences for your loss. That was a terrible thing, and I apologize for jumping into our conversation without first acknowledging your loss."

"Well, thank you for that. And no apology is necessary. I understand the job you have to do." Fels paused and sipped his coffee, waiting for the agent to continue. So far, nothing had aroused his interest.

"When I was made aware of your work, I followed it closely for two reasons. First, I had to be concerned that you would not compromise our work at the BOI. And secondly, I needed to know what valuable information you might have uncovered that might be useful to us."

"And?" Fels interrupted.

"Through your efforts, we have confirmation of some suspicions we've had. This has proven quite useful to the Bureau."

"I'm glad to hear that."

Now Agent Blackmon interrupted Fels. "Detective Krieger, I want you to know that I have used my resources at the BOI to investigate the explosion that killed your family."

Fels winced at the words, but the agent continued speaking.

"Every lead we've followed has turned to a dead end. Initially, some suspected the Black Hand, but we ruled them out early in our investigation. Detective Krieger, I am convinced this wasn't the Italian Mafia's act of revenge for your arrests."

Fels offered cautiously, "I have to agree with you from my point of view. There is something else going on here." He was not sure where the agent was going with this.

"Have you considered all possible arrests and convictions that could lead to a desire for revenge?"

I'm not new to the detective business, Agent Blackmon, he thought. "Yes, I have. There were a few possible suspects, but all of their alibis checked out." Fels did not want to share the details of the current developments in his investigation. His uncertainty about the man's motives persisted. And even if they were intended to assist him, Fels didn't need the BOI stepping in to take over.

"Look, Fels ... may I call you Fels?"

Fels shrugged and nodded. There was no reason for him to cease engagement with the agent yet. But he wanted to know his real reason for this meeting.

"I'm ready to assist you in any way possible. I have resources available at the Bureau that you might not have in Tonawanda."

"I appreciate the offer." Fels looked down at the coffee cup between his hands, then he lifted his eyes. "I'm grateful to know that you've been working to resolve this ... this horrible matter."

"Fels, I know I can't understand what you've gone through. But this is a cowardice attack on the entire law enforcement family. I will do whatever you need. Any time, anywhere." He spoke with sincere eyes and heart to Fels, and Fels recognized it.

Agent Blackmon slid a business card across the table. He kept his eyes fixed on Fels' eyes and emphasized, "Anytime."

With that, Agent Blackmon stood and offered his hand to Fels. Fels looked down at Blackmon's hand, lifted his eyes, and nodded slowly to the agent. The two men shook hands, and Agent Blackmon left the coffee shop. Fels sat pondering the encounter.

The Bureau of Investigation, established within the Department of Justice in 1908, had set up an office in Buffalo in 1911. The Bureau was formed as an independent and more effective investigative arm of federal law enforcement. In particular, the BOI had become focused on the business and banking activities of the Italian Mafia.

The growing presence of the Mafia in Western New York required a need for field agents in this area. Living in Lancaster, New York, just east of Buffalo, Blackmon was tagged to look into the Mafia because of his business accounting background. Blackmon was organized, methodical, and dedicated. In just a few years, he proved himself as a valuable asset to the Bureau.

Myron Blackmon was a likable man who offered his full attention to everyone he met. He respected others who showed a similar commitment to their work. Because of his sincerity in working with others, he had developed good working relationships with local law enforcement agencies in Western New York.

By 1914, Blackmon had already made progress in breaking up some mob activity in Rochester, New York. While his efforts were commendable, he was stifled in his endeavors to get to the mob bosses who insulated themselves from the law through tightly controlled layers of organization. More recently, he was making efforts to look for connections between the Rochester and Buffalo organizations. As best as he could determine, both organizations tiered up to Mafia bosses in New York City.

Fels sipped on a second cup of coffee and mulled over their conversation. He felt the sincerity of the agent. And, while he realized the BOI likely had additional resources, Fels had to proceed on his own with his investigation. In his narrow thinking, Fels felt he owed it to his family to resolve this himself, regardless of what Agent Blackmon might bring to the table.

Fels looked at the agent's business card and placed it in his shirt pocket. He drained the coffee remaining in his cup and left the coffee shop. He had work to do.

CHAPTER 11

It was a cool mid-October Monday morning, cloudy with occasional rain, and quite breezy, when Fels stopped by the 5th Precinct. He wanted to see what information he might find on Sporco, but he was not yet ready to reveal what he had uncovered on his own. He knew the right thing to do was to turn over the information to Chief Bruckhart or Captain Flynn, but Fels was following his instincts at this point. His personal investment in his family's murder influenced his judgment.

With the loss of his family, Fels' heart had grown cold and dry. The only life he felt for the last couple of months was a life bent on finding his family's killer and bringing him to justice. Fels had glimpsed what could be, of what David had talked to him about concerning his purpose. Yes, he had felt a hint of hope from David, but he still felt a stirring toward gaining a revenge for the death of his family. After all, wasn't justice a good thing in the eyes of God?

But at this time, it might be better for Fels to handle justice outside of the court, if necessary. The manner of justice didn't matter to Fels, and the quicker that justice could be administered, the better. In recent weeks, however, Fels was struggling emotionally with his need for vengeance and some sort of softening in his heart that he could not understand. For now, Fels was keeping a calm and rational exterior around the police force.

At the precinct, the chief was out for the day, so Fels stopped by Flynn's office. Fels tapped on the open door to get Flynn's attention. "Captain?"

Flynn looked up from his desk and grinned. "Detective Krieger! How good ta see ya! You're cert'nly lookin' well." Flynn spoke with an Irish brogue. "Come, sit down." Flynn motioned to a padded wooden chair in front of his desk. The captain seemed to have a lighter tone about him than his usual all-business manner.

"Thank you, sir." Fels was always polite and formal with the captain.

"What brings ya by? Ya still have a few more weeks afore the doc said ya'd be ready ta return ta duty. I don't want ya back here until the doc approves." It was more about the rules than how Fels was progressing in his recovery. That was fine with Fels.

"No, sir, they have not released me to come back yet, but I wanted to stop by for a visit." He felt a tightness in his stomach as he lied to Flynn. "I guess I'm getting eager to return." Fels turned a bit in the chair and rubbed his right leg. "But I still have some work to do on this leg." His leg felt fine.

"Well, keep at it. We want ya back healthy." Flynn paused and a serious look came upon his face. "Tell me, Fels, how're ya doin' with the loss of yer family? Again, I'm just so sorry, and I hope I'm not scratchin' a wound not yet closed."

"Oh, no, sir. I'm still working through the entire incident." Fels struggled for strength and composure but did not show it to Flynn. "It's a process, and I still miss them terribly." His insides churned with his words.

"I'm sure, I'm sure." Flynn was not sure what to say next. "What can I do for ya today?"

"Nothing really. As I said, I just stopped in for a brief visit." *And, to see what I can find out about Sporco*, Fels thought to himself.

"Well, Fels, I'm sure yer curious about updates on yer case. I'm afraid we still have no leads. We've followed up on every arrest ya've made, and we have nothin' ta show for it. The men are workin' the streets, but so far there're no leads there either. This just makes little sense, but, of course, we're not givin' up!" Flynn's Irish voice rose to emphasize his point that the case was still very active.

It was just as Fels had expected. From the information he had gleaned from Mosher, he knew there was nothing to be found in Tonawanda or Buffalo. The culprit was in Niagara Falls. The net had not been expanded, and Fels heard nothing to indicate that it would be. Fels was not ready to give his findings over to the captain. He knew in his mind that it would be the right thing to do, but he had already decided he was going to do this on his own.

"Sir, I have great appreciation for the efforts of the men. I'd be pleased if you'd let them know that." Fels pushed himself out of the chair, placing a greater amount of his weight on his left leg. "It's time for me to be on my way. I have to get to my rehabilitation at Turners."

"Fels, I'll pass on yer message ta the men. We look forward ta havin' ya back when yer ready." He reached out his hand to Fels. They shook hands, and Fels left the room limping as the captain advised, "Keep yer collar up. It's a might chilly today."

No leads. About what I expected. Fels knew that corruption ran high and deep in the nearby Buffalo Police Department. His refusal to take part was common knowledge to all, and surely the mob was aware of it. If the mob had any information that could help Fels, they would keep it to themselves.

Fels began forming a plan in his mind. His destination was Niagara Falls. He'd visit some taverns near the Carborundum Company to see if he could discover the whereabouts of Paul Sporco. He'd locate Sporco's residence and use the detective's most valuable asset—he would watch and wait.

It didn't take Fels long to find someone who knew Sporco. The few who acknowledged knowing the man told Fels he was a hot-head. Some even described him as a "nut case." It was amusing to Fels that to a man, they all asked him not to mention that they had talked about him. There seemed to be a common fear of Sporco.

Fels located a tenement on Allen Avenue where Sporco lived. With his motorcycle, Fels could be in the area from his own apartment in about twenty minutes. Over the next few days, Fels rode his motorcycle to the south side of Niagara Falls, where Sporco's tenement was located. He then proceeded on foot to surveil the tenement. It only took a few days to determine the pattern of Sporco's coming and going. Sporco seemed to be lying low as he came straight home after work most days and rarely left his apartment. Sporco had a roommate, and they worked the same shift at the Carborundum Company. Fels would be able to get into the apartment and search for evidence while they were at work.

On two evenings that week, Fels observed two other men visit Sporco's apartment. It seemed odd for someone who was trying to keep a low profile. And, it seemed odd for a working man to have a pattern of visitors on two evenings in one week after work. Maybe they were just meeting for drinks, but Fels' instincts told him there was more to it. He needed to find out why they were meeting.

The following Tuesday, Fels was in place just outside the tenement, sitting on the front steps a few doors down. He was dressed in the manner of a lower class working man, and he had a bottle of gin in his hands. His hat was pulled down over his eyes with just enough of a gap to allow him to observe the area. The collar placed up on his coat was appropriate for the crisp day.

Right on time, the two men arrived, walking from the north. One man had a package in his hands. They entered the front door without pause, just as if they lived in the building. Fels waited a few moments to give them time to get to Sporco's apartment on the second floor. He then entered the building and proceeded up two flights of stairs. Pausing momentarily at the top of the stairs, Fels looked stealthily down the hallway. He knew Sporco was in apartment 5B at the rear of the building. Remaining still, Fels carefully listened for any signs of activity. Hearing none, he stepped softly down the hall until he came to the door marked 5B.

He was cautious not to stand directly in front of the door. Leaning forward to place his ear against the door, Fels listened intently. The sound of chairs sliding and some movement in the room reached his ears. There was some chatter and brief laughter before the tone turned more serious. Fels strained to hear the conversation as the men were keeping their voices low.

"I'll get them ...." Muffled footsteps.

"... well-hidden ..." More footsteps. Then the sound of papers being shuffled. From the sound of the papers being handled, it seemed they might be large papers, but not as thin as newspaper.

"... plans of each turbine room ..."

"... but how? ... tightly locked up ..." More shuffling.

"These are the keys?!" They spoke the words louder than the low volume of the previous conversation.

"... the Welland Canal at the same time." The words were muffled once again.

Fels was wondering if a robbery was being planned. But what did turbines and the Welland Canal have to do with it? The next door in the hallway opened. Fels took two quick small steps backwards away from the door and then shuffled and staggered down the hallway. A lady glanced at Fels, then closed her door.

Fels stood still for a moment, then he returned to 5B. He then heard a word that made the hair on his neck stand, "... the dynamite."

"Of course. You'll have everything ... tell me how much you need ... blow the turbines, and I'll see that you get it."

The room then went quiet for a moment before Fels heard, "Are you expecting anyone?"

"No."

"Did you hear someone outside the door?"

Fels heard a chair slide, and he scurried quietly down the hall to the stairs. He waited there as he heard the door open. There were no footsteps, then the door closed. Fels thought it best not to return to the hall. He went down the stairs and out the front door. He sat back down on the steps with his bottle of gin in view and feigned to be asleep. After another twenty minutes, the two men left the apartment. They looked about the street before stepping away. Neither man seemed concerned about Fels' presence. As the men walked away, Fels observed that neither man had the package they had arrived with. Whatever they came with was now in Sporco's apartment.

Fels felt he was onto something big, but he needed more specifics to determine exactly what was going on. As the two men headed north on 24th Street, Fels decided to follow. He replaced his hat with another, straightened his coat and tie, and ditched the water-filled gin bottle.

He followed the men to a tavern three blocks north at the corner of Falls Street. He waited a few minutes before entering under the sign that simply said "Shorty's." Keeping his eyes straight ahead, he proceeded directly to the bar and ordered a beer. As he tipped his glass, he looked in the mirror behind the bar and saw the two men at a corner table with one other man.

It was obvious from his attire and demeanor that the third man was in charge of whatever the scheme was. He appeared to be about fifty years old. He was well-dressed and had not removed his hat. A fine gold chain crossed his vest to a pocket where he carried his watch. His shirt collar was clean and well-starched. He sat very straight in his chair with his large belly pressed tightly against the dining table. He seemed to need an extra breath from time to time, likely because of his size. As he spoke, he removed a handkerchief from his pocket and wiped his brow.

There was a small fireplace burning near where the men were seated. It was risky, but Fels decided to warm himself by the fire. With his beer in hand, he walked casually across the wooden floor and stopped in front of the fireplace. He reached out one hand toward the fire and glanced over at the table where the three men were looking at him. Fels smiled at the men and nodded his head to them. They responded only by lowering their heads and lowering the volume of their voices.

Fels knew better than to overstay his visit to the fire, so he warmed his backside for a minute and returned to the bar. He did not pick up on much of the conversation, but he gleaned one interesting fact—the men were all speaking German. And, he also overheard one man from Sporco's apartment refer to the older man as Max.

Fels engaged in small talk with the bartender, who spoke with a German accent, and learned that the founder of the establishment had been a James Short.

He had been a Civil War veteran who opened the tavern not long after the war. He had died two years ago, and the new owner kept the original name. Fels took his time finishing his beer, but he did not want to push for more information, as he was concerned about arousing any suspicions. He then thanked the bartender with a small tip, and left, returning south on 24th Street.

There was a heavy German population in Niagara Falls and the surrounding area, but few younger men spoke German in public. And, with the potential for America to enter the war against Germany, most Germans went out of their way not to speak their native tongue. It was unusual for Fels to hear the men conversing in such a manner. Fortunately, he could understand German and speak it, although no longer fluently. He had picked up a few words in his brief encounter with the men in the tavern.

Some of what he heard was confirmation of the suspicions he had gleaned from his surveillance at Sporco's apartment. He overheard a reference to the plans of the power-generating stations and a mention of money to proceed. Something was going to take place at one or more of the electric generating plants, and explosives were certainly involved. He also recalled the reference to the not-too-distant Welland Canal. Fels had to find out what type of action was being planned. He would need to return to Sporco's tenement and search his room.

CHAPTER 12

In the town of Niagara Falls, Paul Sporco kept a low profile by remaining in his shared apartment in a small tenement building on Allen Avenue. He had even avoided going to work for several weeks, but he had returned, for he couldn't risk losing his job and his apartment. His actions had forced him to stay out of sight as much as possible. He was, however, beginning to feel that enough time had passed to clear him of any danger. If they had seen him, surely someone would have come forward by now.

His plan to prove his worth and gain entry into the mob had failed, and failed badly. His actions had made him the subject of a murder investigation by the Tonawanda and Buffalo Police Departments. Fortunately for him, the police focused on the Buffalo and Tonawanda areas, and they apparently lacked a good description of their suspect. So far, the investigation had not included the city of Niagara Falls. The authorities were quite sure that the bomb had to have been placed by someone in the Buffalo area, likely someone from the victim's past. While Sporco had been caught up in the web of the Buffalo Police, as were the others, they set

Sporco free thanks to the criminal influence within the Buffalo Police Department. So, he had no arrest record in Buffalo. He was not likely on any suspect list. Still, he had kept off the streets as much as he could over the past month-and-a-half.

Two days after the explosion at Detective Krieger's home, while feeling his pride at the job he had done, Sporco learned that not only had he not killed Detective Krieger, but he had killed the detective's wife and two children. It devastated him that he had been unsuccessful. Sure, there had been a possibility of collateral damage, but he had not expected these results. However, he felt no remorse for the wife or the children; his only grief was with his failure to execute his mission to impress the mob. Worst of all, however, Detective Krieger was alive!

He also heard a report from his roommate, Robert Werner, that the reason for the blast being larger than expected was that his dynamite had been placed next to a recently filled coal bin. It was sloppy, and Sporco knew it. He might explain it away as part of the plan, but the collateral damage was a real problem. Instead of displaying his experience and expertise with explosives, he had appeared to be nothing more than an undisciplined amateur. It was the type of mistake that someone he was hoping to impress with his skills could not overlook. His hopes to be held in high esteem by the mob were completely dashed.

The mob had no problem with killing when it was necessary. And, often, the more brutal the act, the better. However, and Sporco knew this, family was not to be touched. Women and children were strictly to be left out of any assault against an enemy. Sporco had no chance of ever being part of the mob now. His failure devastated him.

The police did not yet have his name; they only had a description of him from someone who had seen him walking near the old milk barn prior to the explosion. Fortunately for Sporco, the description was rather general and vague in nature. Still, he was keeping to himself as much as he could.

Werner was aware of the situation, and he was keeping Sporco apprised of any activity by the police. Two full weeks after the incident, there were still no suspects named. Now, over two months later, the trail seemed to have gone dry. Sporco was finally able to relax.

Sporco and Werner had both developed their own particular skills while raising themselves on the streets of Buffalo. They had each supplemented their meager incomes by increasingly larger burglaries. Having begun their criminal careers in petty theft, they had expanded into robbing larger businesses in and around Buffalo. Still, they were not making the money that they had thought they would. Their expectations grew with each job.

Sporco had a keen interest in explosives, and that was what he saw as his way out of his present situation and into the "good life." He had proven his abilities to force open any safe they had so far encountered. A few times, Paul had nearly killed himself and others with too large of an explosive charge, but it was all just part of the job to him. He valued himself quite highly and looked at every job as a learning experience. So far, he had proved his worth—and he had killed no one.

Paul aspired to gain entry into the mob. The mob boss, Giuseppe DiCarlo, had full control of the mob activities in the Buffalo area by 1911. In his time, DiCarlo organized the many gangs who operated independently, and often took part in gang wars with one another. With DiCarlo's organization, there was more peace and more money to be made by everyone. He was especially influential in the labor rackets at the docks. He controlled the entire Italian district of Buffalo. With the area serving as a gateway between the U.S. and Canada, Buffalo became a key city for the New York Mafia under DiCarlo's leadership.

Since he did not have the family connections to become part of the local mob, Sporco decided to prove his way in. As most residents of the area knew, the mob had suffered a loss last year when a local police detective broke a big case, incriminating several mobsters of mid-level rank. They were upset by what had transpired, as they were well-connected within the Buffalo Police Department. The mob, in their manner of thinking, had been betrayed.

Detective Felsen Krieger now had a target on his back, with only a small group of law enforcement officers willing to stand with him. Sporco saw this as a great opportunity for himself. If he could take out Detective Krieger using his skills with explosives, he felt he could prove himself as a reliable asset to the mob. He saw it as simple work, almost too easy, in his mind. It was certainly easier than pulling out a gun and shooting someone in the street.

When Sporco was not working at his day job at the Carborundum Company, he watched Detective Krieger's movements. He eventually saw a pattern to the detective's life that brought him home in the early evening, where he spent time after supper reading the newspaper while enjoying a cigar at the rear of his house. Most evenings at this time, his wife would take the children to the upstairs front of the house for a bath. It would be an ideal time to detonate some dynamite, instantly killing the detective. The blast would make a statement that could not be ignored.

So, Sporco planted some dynamite near a rear basement window. He ran the primer cord along a row of bushes from the rear of the house out toward an old milk barn. There was a dirt and gravel alley between the house and the barn where Sporco buried the primer cord just below the surface so it could not be seen.

Sporco arrived early in the morning and spent the entire day in the old barn. He felt assured that no one had seen him in the early hour. He waited until evening when Detective Krieger came home. From the barn, Sporco could see through a window at the rear of the house. When he saw the detective in that window, he knew he could detonate the dynamite.

After waiting for half-an-hour, Sporco saw the detective turn toward the rear. He waited just a moment and then pressed the plunger on the detonator. Nothing happened. He pulled the plunger up and pressed it down again. Still nothing. He checked the connections on his detonator. They were fine. So, he tried the plunger once again. Still nothing. Sporco threw his hat on the barn floor in disgust. *How could I have made a mistake?* He tried the plunger a fourth time after again checking the connections. The results were no different.

He knew he would have to check the connections at the house. He did not like exposing himself, but it was twilight by now, and he hoped no one would spot him. After waiting several minutes, he carefully exited the barn on the side near the line of shrubbery. He kept low and visually inspected the cord as he went. In the alley, he pulled the cord out of the ground where he had covered it with enough dirt and gravel to hide it. He did not see any problems with the cord itself.

As he neared the house, he kept the cord in his hands, ensuring its integrity as he moved along. He arrived at the house after a few minutes, and he found the problem. The cord had pulled out of the dynamite blasting cap. He was furious with himself. How could I have let this happen?! He replaced the cord and double-checked his work. He reminded himself that from now on, he would check and recheck everything. At the back of the house, he stopped momentarily and listened for any activity. He heard none. He assumed that was a good thing. The detective was likely sitting reading the paper, and the rest of the family was likely upstairs. He did not know that Detective Krieger had left the house and that his wife and children were making a final cleaning of the dining room table before returning to the kitchen to finish their work there. Sporco looked over his work one last time before he was ready to return to the barn. He did not notice that next to the basement window was the coal chute.

Sporco stooped low and worked his way slowly back to the old barn. He took his place behind a small cement wall and pressed the plunger. The explosion was deafening, and Sporco heard what appeared to be an almost instantaneous secondary explosion.

His work was done. He did not want to wait around any longer. As he prepared to leave, he saw the result of his work. He did not quite understand when he saw the extent of the blast. Pieces of debris were falling on the old barn and across the alley. The damage was far greater than what he had expected. But he could not stay around any longer. He left through the rear of the barn and disappeared into the night.

CHAPTER 13

Sporco was still cautious, but maybe more so sullen as time passed. While at work in late September, Werner pulled Sporco aside in the lunchroom. "Paul, I have something that might interest you." He kept his voice low and looked around to be sure no one might overhear their conversation. He was a nervous type, and while his intent was to be discrete, his manner was anything but. However, most everyone kept to themselves, or a small tight-knit group, and no one paid any attention to the two men.

Sporco had been both on edge and a bit broody at the same time since his failed job. He had every hope of being accepted by the mob, but his mistake had instead made him an outcast to the organization. He had displayed a lack of understanding of their inner traditions, and he had made a grave error with the force of the explosion. How was he to have known about the coal delivery, and how that would affect the explosiveness?

On top of that was the fact that his misstep, as he liked to refer to it, was under investigation by the law. So far, there were no clues leading the police to him, but he was still watching his back. He was feeling sorry for himself, and only himself. The fact that he had killed the detective's entire family was not his real concern. That was only a mistake. Why couldn't the organized crime leaders understand that and see what he had to offer?

Sporco's response to Werner was one one of distant disinterest. "Yeah, what's that?"

"A couple of guys I know on the loading dock would like to meet you. They're good German men who are looking for someone with your, uh, talents." Werner displayed excitement in an attempt to arouse Sporco's interest. He looked at Sporco, waiting for a response, but Sporco barely moved.

"So. What's it about?" Sporco did not even look up from the sandwich in his hands.

"Look, Paul, I think you need to hear it from them. They want to meet tonight. I told them you didn't go out much and that they could come over." He now spoke with a sense of urgency, wanting Sporco to feel the same.

"Whadda they wanna talk to me about?" Sporco appeared annoyed about the whole thing.

"Paul, I already told them to come over, so just listen to what they have to say. Do that for me, will ya?" His tone was now pleading.

Sporco finally raised his head. "Sure."

They finished their lunches in silence and went back to work.

That evening, two men arrived at the tenement. They entered the apartment, and Werner introduced the two, Peter Niemand and Otto Bergmann. Peter Niemand was a little larger than Sporco, a man with a large build himself. Niemand had a face like a bulldog and a broad neck atop broad shoulders. Otto Bergmann was just a little bigger than Werner, a small, wiry guy. Bergmann was a timid man with slouched shoulders holding up a head that seemed too large for his body. Niemand was obviously a few years older than the other three men. Sporco and Bergmann both sported mustaches.

After cautious introductions, the four men sat at a small table in the main living area of the apartment. Sporco seemed as disinterested as he had been at lunch. Because of Sporco's attitude, Werner was uneasy and squirmed in his chair. Having gone this far, he had to see that this worked out for both him and Sporco.

Werner managed to break the ice. "Paul, here, he's real anxious to hear what you guys have to say. I haven't really told him anything—just like you asked." He tried to look Peter Niemand in the eyes, but he found he could not. Niemand's piercing blue eyes had a force of their own that Werner could not bring himself to engage. The room became uncomfortably silent.

Niemand broke the silence. "Glad to hear that, but Paul doesn't appear to be all that interested."

"Oh, no, he's just tired." Werner tried to cover for Sporco.

"I can talk for myself!" Sporco sat up tall and loudly interrupted. "You're here. I'm here. So tell me what this is all about!" With feigned interest he said, "I can hardly wait to hear." He sat back in his chair and folded his arms.

Niemand interjected, "Maybe this was a mistake. Let's go, Otto."

"No! Wait. I'm sure Paul will be interested once he hears some details." Werner was trying to save the meeting. After all, he knew there was likely a big payday involved.

Sporco looked at Niemand and made a gesture of tipping a hat toward him. "As I said, since we're all here, I'm ready to listen. So go ahead."

Niemand sighed before speaking. "Okay. We're aware of your, uh, special talents, Paul. We have a project that could use someone with those talents, and we're hoping you might be interested." He paused momentarily before continuing. "You would be paid well. Very well. Well enough that you could leave this area and start over somewhere new where no one would know you. I think you understand what I'm saying."

Sporco was once again sitting up straight in his chair and leaning forward, but this time it was with real interest. "Yes, Mr. Niemand, you do have my interest." Sporco envisioned leaving the Niagara Falls and Buffalo areas to get away from the continuing investigation into the bombing of Detective Krieger's house and the killing of his family. He saw a sense of safety in being able to leave the area. And, enough money to start over?! That was simply the icing on the cake.

"Good. Now, before we continue, I have to have your oath to me that regardless of the outcome of tonight's discussion, neither of you will say anything about this to anyone." His face was stern and cold. It was obvious this was a serious matter. His steel eyes shifted to each of the men.

"You obviously know what I've done. I am in no position to tell anyone anything. And, I'm sure Robert agrees, don't you, Robert?"

Werner looked around the table and nodded his head. "Of course." He was in it for the money, so swearing to a silence that he would have kept anyway was no big deal to him.

Niemand again took control of the discussion. "You are both men of good German heritage, are you not?" Niemand was actually smiling, as Sporco and Werner nodded their heads in agreement. "That's very important. Very important! You see, many of us Germans still have family in the homeland. Family that we love, and family that is in need of our support." His icy eyes slowly changed to glowing, caring eyes.

Sporco was beginning to imagine in his mind a large heist that would provide money for families in Germany. He was alright with that—as long as he received the large share promised to him. Money always made everything right in his mind. With this much concern for silence, he imagined it must be a large payoff.

Werner interrupted, "Well, the United States is sure not helping Germany. Wilson's trying to keep us out of the war, but his lack of action, or his action to support Great Britain, is only making it more difficult for the average German citizen."

Niemand was now encouraging. "Exactly, Robert! In fact, Wilson seems to be leaning toward joining the war on the side of Great Britain. I predict he'll do just that by next year. That's why we need to act now!"

There was a contagious excitement filling the room. Sporco was rising off his chair as he spoke. "This must be a big heist if you think it's going to have a great impact for the German people! I'm all in! Let's talk about the details!"

Niemand looked squarely at Sporco. "This is much bigger than a heist, Paul. Much bigger! What we are planning will slow the ability of Wilson to provide direct support to Great Britain and their allies." Niemand continued, "We are going to impact industry in a way that will stop the flow of goods to Great Britain." Niemand sat tall and proud in his chair.

Sporco was becoming a bit confused. "But where's the big payout I plan to get? You're talking about interrupting goods and services. How does that pay out? Why do you need my services?"

"This is about more than the money, Paul. Again, this is about helping the struggling German people." Niemand continued his appeal to German unity.

"And, just how is it I get paid—uh—we get paid?" Sporco's only genuine concern was a big payout for himself.

"We will pay you. We're part of a large organization that is very well-funded. This isn't a heist, as you say, rather your services will support our plan, and we will pay you well. It's all very simple, really." Niemand was again smiling with his penetrating blue eyes.

Sporco's face contorted more to one side than usual. His nostrils were flaring. "Let's get to the point. What is it we're actually doing?"

"Remember your oath to me." It was more a threat than a reminder. Niemand again looked carefully into the eyes of each man. "Paul, we need your services to blow up the electric turbines along the Niagara River." He watched Sporco and Werner as their eyes widened. They had not made Werner aware of these details, and he was as shocked as Sporco.

"Blow the turbines?! How can ... I mean ... what ...." Sporco could not express a thought.

"Yes, blow the turbines!" Niemand's eyes glared with a twisted sense of joy.

After being assured that the two men were in on the scheme, Niemand laid out the plan to Sporco and Werner. "I work for a man named Max. You don't need to know anymore about him for now. Max has connections at the highest levels of the German military command. He is a businessman who can get necessary supplies into the country through his connections. I report directly to Max, and he has given me the authority to organize a small group to carry out a very important piece of a larger project. The overall goal is to disrupt any support that America could be ready to provide to Great Britain. By doing this, we will give the German people the support and hope they need to defend themselves from the imperialist empires."

Niemand paused and evaluated the men. They were providing their rapt attention. He was pleased and continued, "While I have not been provided any details, there are other projects underway that will take place simultaneously with ours." He continued sharing what information he could for the time being.

Niemand was generally aware of many of the other plans, but he was not in contact with any of those who were leading the groups that were undertaking the other actions. This made him feel a part of a much larger objective and boosted his ego since he felt trusted with such information.

When all of this was tied together with providing aid to the poor German people who were being cut off from supplies by the allied countries, the German men found it easy to defend any actions of such a plan, including the possibility of death. Of course, Sporco had already demonstrated his own willingness to kill to advance his own position.

Niemand began providing an overview of the plot to blow the turbines. The events would take place in late November, providing ample time for the men to put a detailed and flawless plan together. Sporco would be responsible for providing the explosive charges with the assistance of Werner. Sporco would need to be able to put together timed explosives so that a number of bombs could be deployed to explode at the same time. Sporco had been expanding his skills, and such a device would not present any difficulties for him.

Niemand would provide diagrams and plans of the turbine power plants for the two men. With other men who were working in the powerstations, they would know exact build specifications for the turbines so that appropriate explosive charges could be deployed. Niemand would ensure access at entry points and an escape route upon completion of their mission.

After laying out the high-level plan, Niemand asked if there were any questions or concerns. Sporco spoke up. "It sounds like I will require a substantial amount of dynamite. I don't have access to the quantity required, and I can't place myself out in the open to source the dynamite." He stopped there, unable to offer a solution.

Niemand answered, "We have the dynamite sourced for you. All you and Werner need to do is put the bombs together. I'll have specific information on your requirements when we next meet. Is there anything else?"

Sporco replied, "No," and everyone else nodded their heads.

Niemand arranged the next meeting at another location. Max had a place where they could meet without arousing any suspicions. At the next meeting, he would provide diagrams of the targeted turbines. Sporco and Werner must assure that all the written plans and diagrams would be kept secure and out of sight while they used the plans to determine the best areas for maximum effectiveness of the explosives.

Sporco had a perfect place to keep the plans hidden. He had used it to hide away money from his burglaries. Burglaries seemed so small compared to this. His payout would assure his ability to escape the area forever and begin anew on his own. And he would make a name for himself. He could see a day when he would be lauded for his efforts to help the poor Germans in the homeland. Sure, he would have to lie low for some time, but he could foresee a day when he would have it all.

Sporco could not remove the perverse smile from his face as the other men left the apartment. Emboldened by the role he was to play, Sporco dropped his guard and left his apartment more frequently. The police still had no solid leads on the killer, and Sporco saw no reason to stay hidden.

CHAPTER 14

Fels arrived in Sporco's neighborhood in mid-after-noon. He entered the building without hesitation, just as if he lived there. Sporco and his roommate would be at work for at least another few hours, providing Fels plenty of time to search the room.

Fels climbed the stairs and picked up his pace to apartment 5B, observing his surroundings the entire time. The hallways were clear and quiet. The cheap warded door lock was easy for Fels to defeat. Fels opened the door, entered quickly while looking about the hall-way, and closed the door behind him. He then re-locked the door.

The quarters were lit by a single window across the room on what would be the alley side of the building. A simple, dirty curtain was pulled to one side, allowing the dim light in. The shadowed alley outside did not let in any direct sunlight. As Fels scanned the room, he heard footsteps in the hallway. He held his breath as he heard someone at the door. The lock was being opened, the door handle turned, and Sporco walked in.

The sight of Fels shocked Sporco. He took a half-step backward in the doorway. "What's going on here?!

You're in the wrong place, buddy!" Sporco started walking toward Fels, then he stopped in his tracks. "Wait, I know you ... damn it!" Sporco threw a chair at Fels and turned and ran out of the room, slamming the door behind him. He had recognized Fels, and immediately figured he had come there to arrest him for killing his family.

Sporco shot out of the building and crossed a vacant lot, making a beeline for the railroad. The rails were busy this time of the day, and he ran to hop aboard the train on the nearby tracks. It was the simplest way to an easy escape.

The chair knocked Fels off balance, causing him to fall to the floor, while Sporco fled with a good head start. Exiting the building into a sudden burst of rain, Fels looked about from the doorway to locate Sporco. He looked up and down Allen Avenue, expecting to see Sporco running to the east or the west. It was when a train whistle caught Fels' attention that he saw Sporco about to catch up to the train across the distant field. There was no way Fels was going to catch him before he could board the slow-moving train that was gaining speed.

Fels ran about a block-and-a-half to retrieve his motorcycle. The only possible way for Fels to catch the train was on his motorcycle. The now-heavy rain would make the ride difficult, but it was the only chance Fels had of catching Sporco. He knew that if he did not catch him, Sporco would disappear from the area. Fels was not about to let that happen; he wanted Sporco to pay for what he had done.

The motor sputtered to life behind the shed where Fels had left it. Donning a pair of riding goggles, Fels rode down a cinder alley to a road filling with pools of water. There was no chance of riding across the field that

Sporco had crossed. Fels would have to ride on the road parallel to the tracks to catch the train.

He made a right turn onto Buffalo Street, sliding in the rain-soaked, and now slippery, roadway. Regaining control of his Harley-Davidson, Fels increased the throttle until he was traveling forty-five miles per hour. The rain stung his face. The rain drops streamed and smeared across his goggles, and he had to lift one hand to clear the lenses so he could see. At the same time, he was watching the train to his left. It wouldn't be long before the train would cross Buffalo Street in front of him. With the tracks making a slight curve where it crossed the street, at least it would not be increasing its speed. But Fels felt it was traveling fast enough that Sporco would not be jumping off.

Fighting the rain and struggling to see, Fels and the train approached their intersection. Fels knew he would not beat the train. He dropped the throttle and began applying the brakes, which unfortunately did not perform well in the wet conditions. Fels had only one move to make. He turned toward the grassy area on the roadside and laid the motorcycle down on its left side. Fels held on as best as he could until the motorcycle came to a stop at a small rise on the side of the road.

The train passed by as Fels struggled to get to his feet. He looked up at the train as it passed. It was one of the regular passenger trains. There in a window in the last car was Sporco laughing as the car disappeared into the heavy rainfall.

Fels knew the train would make a stop just opposite the falls near First Street. If he could get his motorcycle started, he had a chance of reaching the train as it stopped. He cleaned wet sod out of the motorcycle and tried to get it started. After several attempts, the engine sputtered, chugged hard, and sputtered again to life. Once again, Fels hit full throttle and was back on Buffalo

Street. The street and the tracks no longer ran parallel, so Fels had to make a right turn onto 4th Street. He nearly lost the motorcycle from under him, but he managed to recover and continue.

The deluge of rain now turned into a steady, moderate rain. After a moment, Fels could see the train just a block-and-a-half away. It was slowing, but it had not yet stopped. Fels might just get there in time to apprehend Sporco.

Fels was now less than a block away. The train had stopped, and passengers were disembarking. *No, I can't be too late! He must be in the small crowd*. Fels stopped in the road and scanned the area, looking for Sporco. He drove slowly up to the stopped train. *Sporco has to be here!* He drove back down to the last car on the train. It appeared everyone had gotten off. There was a conductor standing at the door of the car.

Fels called out to him, "I'm Detective Krieger. I'm looking for a suspect who was on this car. Has everyone gotten off?"

"There's no one left on this car, detective."

The conductor was of no further assistance despite Fels' description of Sporco. Hoping to glimpse Sporco, Fels drove past each of the four passenger cars, but there was no sight of him. Fels was discouraged, but he was not giving up. He stopped his motorcycle and dashed up to each of the remaining three cars to see if Sporco had entered one of them. He was not there. Still, he had to be nearby.

He stopped to ask some passengers who were waiting under their umbrellas in the rain. He described Sporco and told them he might have been in a hurry. His luck turned around when a man reported seeing someone who fit Sporco's description. He was definitely in a hurry, running down Falls Street toward the falls. Fels thanked the man and returned to his motorcycle.

Again, with some difficulty, the engine hesitated and came to life. Fels proceeded down Falls Street, looking down each cross street as he went. Arriving at Riverside Street, Fels felt an apprehension that he had lost the killer of his family.

Turn left, Fels.

The voice was right next to him as he sat at the intersection, but no one was there. A right turn would take him toward the International Bridge to Ontario. It would make sense for the killer to attempt an escape across the bridge to Canada. Fels turned his handlebars to the right as he prepared to head toward the bridge.

Fels, you need to turn to the left!

It was Marie's voice! Fels was confused. "Marie, is that you? Where are you?!"

But now there was nothing but silence. He didn't understand. Then, a burst of lightning revealed someone standing in the rain with a bicycle. With a hat pulled down low on his brow, he was throwing his right arm out emphatically, pointing down the road toward Niagara Falls.

Fels moved his handlebars to the left and turned onto Riverside, approaching the turnoff to the footbridge to Green Island. It was at that moment that the Harley-Davidson gasped and stalled. Fels tried to start the machine with no success. The rain had likely created too many problems for the engine.

As Fels looked off into the distance in frustration, he saw a figure dash across the street and onto the footbridge to Green Island. Fels struggled to see clearly as he began running toward the bridge that spanned what was known as Hell's Half Acre, the violent rapids upstream of the American side of Niagara Falls. The figure turned to look at Fels, and Fels confirmed it was Sporco.

As Fels entered the bridge, he saw a sign indicating that the bridge was closed for repair. He jumped over a small gate and onto the bridge in pursuit of Sporco. He felt close to achieving the goal of bringing his family's killer to justice.

Sporco fell into an area of repair as he neared the end of the bridge. Fels made note of the location. At the end of the bridge, Sporco was now climbing over a closed gate in the darkening late day. He hit the ground and headed along the shoreline. As Fels jumped the same gate, he saw Sporco slip down the embankment and into the churning water. Fels grabbed a downed branch and ventured into the turbulent waters to rescue Sporco, who was being swiftly pulled into the rapids. Sporco reached for the branch. His hands swept across the leaves at the end of the branch, but gaining no hold, he was pulled out into deeper water. With his own footing giving way, Fels struggled to get back to the shoreline.

Sporco was now caught in the rapids of Hell's Half Acre. Fels could not hear his screams above the roar of the water. He saw a raised hand as Sporco disappeared in the distance and headed to his death in the torrents of water about to carry him over the American Falls.

Fels suddenly found himself in the same predicament as Sporco. He looked about in a panic. As the river current pulled him from shore, his foot became entangled in something on the river bottom. His foot slipped deeper into an opening, pulling Fels beneath the surface.

Fels flashed back to a childhood memory of losing himself beneath the surface of the pond when he became entrapped in the muck. He remembered his panic and his loss of consciousness. At that moment, he felt something hit his shoulder. He grabbed for the object, getting a firm grip on what seemed to be a branch. His head popped to the surface, and he took a deep breath. His foot was free, and he was being pulled toward the shore. In a burst of lightning, Fels saw the young man with the hat who had directed him to the falls.

Pulling himself up on a large rock at the shoreline, Fels turned back toward the roaring river. "No! This is not what I wanted! I wanted to look you in the eyes and tell you that you would die in the electric chair! I wanted you to know about the lives you had taken!" Fels put his head in his hands and cried. In the pouring rain, the deafening whitewater silenced Fels' cries.

Fels, justice has been served. It is God's to take, not yours. We are fine. Be free of this.

Fels turned around, expecting to see Marie. "This was not my imagination. I heard you, Marie! Where are you?! Please, speak to me again!" But Fels only heard the roar of the river and felt the pounding of the rain. "How can I be free?"

Once Fels regained his footing, he looked up to see that the man had turned to leave. Fels called out, "No, don't walk away. I must thank you!"

The young man stopped and turned to face Fels. Fels fixed his eyes in disbelief at the young man, who appeared to be completely dry. Sensing Fels' stare, the young man turned his back to Fels. He took a few steps away from Fels before again turning to face him. Another flash of lightning exposed the young man standing on the riverbank. He was soaked to the bone from the storm, his long brown hair in ringlets covering his face.

Fels was unsure of what he had seen. He quickly told himself the events and the storm and his near-drowning were just playing tricks with his mind.

The man eased down the muddy slope to Fels and reached out his hand to help him up the slippery river bank. As the two moved to safety, Fels extended his hand to the man. "I can't thank you enough. Without your quick thinking, I would have been swept over the falls to my death."

The man replied, "I was fortunate to be nearby."

"Well, I must say, I was the fortunate one."

The man merely smiled politely at Fels. Considering the circumstances, his calm demeanor through the events struck Fels. Fels himself felt a calmness sweep over him. The anger he had at losing Sporco was gone. And it wasn't a sense of final vengeance, it was a sense of life to be fully lived. Fels did not understand his feelings. Standing in the chilly rain, Fels felt a warmth and kindness flowing through him.

His thoughts turned to the young man and a need to know him. "Who is it I must thank? I'm Fels Krieger. Well, Detective Fels Krieger. I was in pursuit of a suspected murderer, the man who was swept over the falls." Fels turned momentarily, staring out over the raging waters.

Turning back, Fels said, "You're the young man who was standing at the end of the road pointing in the direction of the falls."

"Yes, I was."

"Why did you do that?"

The young man removed his hat and, with his fingers, he swept his hair back over his head. It was at that moment that Fels recognized the young man. It was David Smith whom he had met at Turners. Fels was stunned by the coincidence.

"Its you, David Smith, from Turners!" A huge smile crossed Fels' face.

The two worked their way back across the bridge together. The storm was now passing, and the rain was much lighter. It would end shortly.

"I could see that you were in pursuit of the other man. I thought I might be of some assistance."

"Well, another thank-you for that. You apparently have pretty good intuition."

"I do, yes."

"And how did you get here so quickly?"

"On my bicycle, of course. I am quite a good bicy-clist." David paused and added, "You are quite experienced on your motorcycle."

"Yes, I do ride it quite a bit, but, David, I must ask you one more thing." The rain had now stopped completely. "You appeared to be dry when you pulled me from the river. Can you explain that?"

Still quiet and polite, the young man said, "I am not sure what you saw." David looked down at his rain-soaked clothing. "But, obviously, I am soaked from the storm."

"It must've been the storm and my near-drowning that played tricks on my mind."

"Yes, I suppose."

Fels shook his head as if to clear his mind.

"David, I know it's getting late, but there's a nearby coffee shop where we could warm up and dry out. Could I at least offer you a cup of coffee for your life-saving efforts?"

"That would be fine. And maybe we could discuss your situation further."

David looked directly in Fels' eyes and, once again, provided Fels a complete sense of comfort and a peace. Fels wondered what he meant about his situation, and the detective in him wanted to uncover the answer.

CHAPTER 15

Fels and David entered the quiet diner not far to their east along Buffalo Street near the Niagara Power Company and Port Day. They had walked to Al's Diner, Fels pushing his motorcycle, and David pushing his bicycle. The diner was a place frequented by the workers at the powerstations. At this hour, it was empty except for an older man seated at the counter and two younger men in a booth near the door.

Fels and David sat at an empty booth near the back door of the diner. Fels experienced an eagerness to learn more about David. But this was not in his usual detective mode of interest. He could feel that warmth and kindness that exuded from David. He seemed to experience this whenever he was in the presence of the young man, and he wanted to know more about that. *Why does he have this effect on me? What's his story?*

A pleasant waitress placed two glasses of water in front of the men and took their order. After she left their booth, Fels spoke. "First of all, once again, thank you for saving me. You need to know how truly grateful I am for what you did for me." Fels extended his hand to David, and the two shook hands across the table. "David, I'd like to know more about you. You were of great help to me, and you showed up at just the right time. What drew you to that area? I mean, it was raining, and there you were with your bicycle."

David's face glowed. "Well, as you know, it had not been raining for that long. I was riding in the area when I saw the man you were chasing. He just looked like someone trying to get away with something. It was my instinct, I suppose."

Fels sipped from the water glass. "You are an incredibly calm person—"

David interrupted, "Fels, I can answer all your questions and more. If you're going to drink some more water, I'd suggest you do it before I begin." David smiled at Fels as if he had a secret he was about to share. He felt it was time to let Fels know everything.

Fels looked puzzled.

"Go ahead, take a drink before I begin." He was still smiling.

Fels lifted his glass to David as if toasting, then took a drink of his water. Fels leaned forward. "Okay, begin."

"Fels, I am here as a messenger—"

"A messenger?"

"Let me finish. I am here as a messenger from God." His eyes studied Fels, searching for the truth of his initial reaction to David's statement.

Fels' face was blank for a moment. Then he spoke, "Well, you have talked a lot like a pastor, but I thought you were too young for that to be the case. At the same time, you do speak with a lot of confidence and maturity for someone your age. Are you with a particular church or denomination?"

David released a soft, polite laugh, preparing to tell Fels he was not quite correct. "No, I am not a pastor. And I am not with any church or denomination. You see, I serve God and only God. I work at His pleasure."

"I don't understand. Are you like a street preacher, then?"

With his calm demeanor and a warm smile, David drew Fels in as he answered. "Fels, I am an angel."

"What?!" Fels looked around as he had spoken loudly. He lowered his tone. "What? An angel? What kind of game are you playing?" Fels kicked into detective mode. "Are you involved with Sporco in some way? I want to know what's going on!" His voice was rising again. Then, he became noticeably calm. It was that warmth and peace that wrapped around him.

"Fels, you feel that flow of stillness, and warmth, and wonder? I have provided that for you." David then extended his right hand out to Fels across the table. "Here, take my hand. Let me show you something. Take my hand and close your eyes." He waited for Fels.

Fels looked into David's eyes with a furled brow, but he reached across the table and took David's hand in his in the manner of a polite handshake.

Out of nowhere, a bright white light enveloped Fels, surpassing any brightness he had ever before witnessed. But as bright as it was, it was not blinding. The very light itself seemed to exude a peace like no other that Fels had ever experienced. It was a light that he could feel penetrating his very being. He felt as if every weight he had ever carried was lifted from him, and he tingled with delight and joy in a way he could not understand. Over a few moments, as he soaked in the healing light, Fels noticed more detail in his surroundings.

Fels then realized that David's voice was coming from a figure that seemed to be made of the light. It was not as bright as the surrounding light, but as bright as it was, Fels could make out some details of the light figure. While the figure looked nothing like David, in his heart, Fels knew it was David.

"Fels, I am an angel of the most high God; I serve Him and Him alone. In this service, I am a messenger sent to work with humankind. And, as you may now likely understand, I have been sent to serve you at God's command."

Fels spoke with wonder. "I have so many questions. But why me?" Fels' mind filled with thoughts of Marie and the children. "Is my family here? Can I see them? Why were they not saved? Are you here to show me my family?" Fels rapidly spat out the words in quick succession before David lifted his large arm, and Fels fell still.

"I understand your questions, and I will explain it all to you. Be patient."

The peace had not left Fels, but his circumstances, and his personality, prompted him with the flood of questions. He felt a sense of patience and calm as he quieted himself to listen as David spoke.

"First, regarding your family. Fels, I am not here to arrange any kind of communication with your family. But I will tell you this: I was present when three other messengers escorted your wife and children to the heavenly realm. They are enjoying the peace of the Kingdom of God that even in your present state here with me, you could not comprehend.

"Fels, you are only seeing a glimpse, a shadow, if you will, of what truly is. This, of course, lets you know that all is well with your wife and children. And, Fels, you will be with them one day. I do not know when that day will be. That is not for either of us to know.

"It was in God's hands to determine their time in the present earthly kingdom. That time is fleeting for all humankind. Your body is a temporary home for the spiritual being that you are and have always been. Once you shed the body, humankind lives as a fully spiritual being in Heaven.

"You see, humans are spiritual beings contained within a body. Angels are simply spiritual beings who do not have bodies. We are neither male nor female. God has created us as spiritual servants. When you leave that body, when you die, you return to your spiritual nature. You will leave this present earth and enter the spiritual realm of heaven at that time.

"One day there will be a new earth. Then, you will receive a new body, but not like the old body you leave behind when you die. You will receive a perfect incorruptible body, the body that Adam had before the fall. All of that is in God's control."

"But if you are a spirit with no body, how—?"

"As a messenger, I can take on a human form to interact with you and with others. It makes it much easier for you, as humankind, to communicate with a ministering spirit.

"Now, not all angels are sent as messengers. Let me tell you about the heavenly host. There are hierarchies of spiritual beings, some being angels like myself. But, you must understand that these are not hierarchies in the manner in which humans think. You see, there is no competition, there is no striving to be something more, there are no status disputes, there is no jealousy. Angels all have the same single purpose: we exist only to fulfill the will of God. And so we serve with the fullness of the spirit of God.

"The hierarchies of spiritual beings exist only to denote the manner in which we serve. Throughout the ages, humans have been given much information about the spiritual beings. Much of this has been retained, but, as humans are, much more has been dismissed as tales, legends, and myths. It is unfortunate that humankind has given away so much of the knowledge and so many of the gifts that have been presented to them by God through the ages. But this is all a grievous part of living in the fallen world.

"Now, for your understanding, here is how we are organized, and you will recognize most of these terms. First, there are the Seraphim. These are the guardians of the Lord's throne. They have no other purpose than praising God and serving in His very presence.

"Next are the Cherubim. These are celestial attendants to God. They are placed at the boundary between the sacred and the profane to protect the Holy from contamination.

"Then there are Thrones who are symbols of God's authority and justice. They are spirits of humility, peace, and submission. These three hierarchies are what many humans refer to as the First Order of Angels. They do not serve as messengers to humankind, they serve only God.

"What humans refer to as the Second Order of Angels are the Dominions, Virtues, and Powers. Dominions have authority over the rest of the angels in lower hierarchies. They also provide power to governing authorities on earth. They help keep the world in proper order. The Virtues work miracles and send down the grace of God to the saints. They also encourage humans to strengthen their faith in God. Then, the Powers are warrior angels who help defend humans against evil. They provide grace and courage to worthy and deserving humans."

Fels found himself captivated by what David was revealing to him. As David paused, Fels realized his surroundings had changed. The bright white had been filled with colors—colors that Fels had never seen. He could not begin to know how to explain these colors to anyone. At the same time, it all seemed familiar with fields and flowers and trees and birds, with a beauty that penetrated to his very core.

David continued, "Finally, the third tier of angels consists of the Principalities, Archangels, and Angels.

The Principalities have command over all the angels below them in the hierarchy. They take care that all divine orders are fulfilled. They watch over earthly kingdoms and lands and raise worthy people to honorable offices. The Archangels act as God's messengers in critical times to deliver important messages to humankind. And, finally, the Angels, such as myself, are the closest to the material world and humankind. We carry prayers to God and deliver God's messages to the people on earth. Of course, it is this angelic position that humankind is most aware of. The others are recognized by their work in service to the Most High God.

"We are often involved with God in his work of the Holy Spirit. We provide opportunities and leadings as necessary for God's callings to be discerned and understood by humankind."

Fels understood every bit of information that David relayed to him. But, it was more than just understanding the words and the ideas, he felt them come alive in him as if he himself had lived in that heavenly space for a time. There was a clarity that went beyond all explanation.

"Then you are a true blessing to us on earth, and I should bow down before you in praise and thanksgiving for your service—"

"No! While I have a greater power than humankind, and while I am a spirit being in God's Heavenly Host, He is the only one due your worship and praise! I serve in honor and glory and praise to the Most High God. You, too, are to give glory and praise to God, and to God alone. Please do not think any praise is deserved by a mere servant of the Holy One."

Fels felt the power of David's words to the very essence of his soul. He understood the humility being expressed by a genuine servant to the one true God of the universe. "I'm sorry. I think I understand now. However, doesn't the power you have place you far above me as a human?"

"No. Once again, you must hear me with no misunderstanding. We angels are servants to God created by God. God also created you humans—in His image. You see, humankind are foremost to God. As angel servants to God, we are also servants to humankind. I am by no means over you; I am here as a servant of God to serve you according to His will. One day when you inherit the Kingdom of God, you will be above the angels. For now, I work in service to you at God's command."

Fels had one additional question building up inside of him. "Can I see my family?"

"Fels, they are spiritual beings in the Kingdom. You are a human being. That is not possible for me to arrange." David paused for a moment. "However, still your mind and think of the love of Marie."

Fels drew in a deep breath and slowly exhaled in the manner George had taught him at Turners. He was suddenly filled with the fullest love he had ever experienced with Marie. He felt her presence within him, and he felt as if he was present within her.

"Fels, be reminded of what God said in the Word, 'Then the Lord God made a woman from the rib he had taken out of the man, and he brought her to the man. The man said, "This is now bone of my bones and flesh of my flesh; she shall be called woman, for she was taken out of man." That is why a man leaves his father and mother and is united with his wife, and they become one flesh.'"

As Fels floated in a love unlike anything he had ever known, David went on, "Of course, oneness in marriage reaches far beyond the physical level. The original Hebrew word translated as flesh refers to much more than your physical nature. It relates to the whole human existence. The Biblical view of one flesh communicates a unity that covers every facet of a couple's combined lives as husband and wife. In marriage, two human lives unite as one emotionally, intellectually, spiritually, and in every other way. They are so close that they function like one person, balancing each other's strengths and weaknesses so that together they can fulfill their God-given calling."

Fels felt every moment of their lives together with that purity of love that is only possible with God's blessing. He saw every minute of their growth together while on earth. He experienced with Marie's spirit sharing every thought, activity, and feeling. Then, as if awakening from a dream, Fels became aware of his presence with David.

"But I have heard Marie's voice. You said we could not communicate, but, David, I have heard her voice." Fels was pleading to understand.

"Fels, you heard nothing but your own thoughts and your own voice. As I said, through marriage, the two of you are one in every way—you function as one. You were expressing words that Marie might say to you in the particular situation. You heard yourself in a manner that Marie might speak to you."

Fels felt like crying, not tears of sadness, but tears of joy. "David, I can't explain the sense of love and hope and joy that I have. Words cannot do it justice. Thank you."

Everything David showed him brought a profound peace to Fels concerning his family. He knew to the core of his being that they were well and thriving as spirit beings in God's kingdom. He knew that one day he would join them. He knew that he and Marie were truly one. She would remain with him in spirit until the day he would join them.

After what seemed like many hours, the light dissipated and Fels opened his eyes, having forgotten that he was at the diner. He reached out for his water glass and found it still cold to the touch. It was as if no time at all had passed. He thought to himself, *Was this some sort of trick, maybe hypnosis?*

David responded to Fels' thoughts, "No, Fels, this was not a trick, not hypnosis, and you know it."

Fels turned his head to the side, and a smile crossed his face. "Yes, I do know it. So tell me, David, why are you here? I mean, why am I so blessed with this knowledge? I know you saved my life, and you have given me a new understanding. But it seems as if there is more than that. I feel like there is something I am called to do. Can you help me with this?"

"Yes, my service is to you. You have been through a very difficult time. I am here to give you encouragement, to give you strength, to help you get refocused, and to assist and protect you as you work to serve and protect others. Fels, do you recall your near-drowning as a boy?"

The event again flashed before Fels' eyes. "Yes, I do. Was—?"

"Yes, that was me that day at the pond."

"Of course!"

"For you, that was so many years ago, but you see, there is no time for God. Remember, He was, He is, and He always will be, the Great I Am. My time with you when you were a child does not differ from my time with you now. Did anyone tell you who pulled you away from the fire?"

"I was only told it was a young man who no one recognized ... and now I know it was you!"

"Yes."

"Okay, then, why are you here at this time for me? I understand the help I needed, and I did need it. So, thank you for that. But what now?"

"Now, I am here to continue providing you encouragement, strength, focus, and protection. As I said, you have a purpose as a law enforcement officer to serve and protect others—to be a peacekeeper. I am here to help you do that. It is as simple as that for me. That is my direction from above."

"So, does that mean I'll make every arrest and lock up every criminal?"

"That is up to you. I will assist you in making moral decisions in pursuing justice with other humankind. I do not know how that will play out in God's plan for you or for others. Remember, everything you do influences someone else. And, remember Jesus' command to all, 'You shall love the Lord your God with all your heart and with all your soul and with all your strength and with all your mind, and your neighbor as yourself.' This is how true justice will be carried out."

"Well, how do I engage you? I mean, is there some secret word I should use to call upon you for help?" He realized that while he thought he understood so much of what David had shown him, he still did not fully understand. He knew how childish his question sounded as soon as the words left his mouth.

David was kind. "No, no code words, Fels. I'll be around when I see the need. You see, although I serve at God's command, He gives us a free will in carrying out His orders, just as you have your free will. My will, however, will never contradict God's will. The manner in which I carry out His command is at my discretion with the breadth of knowledge of the Kingdom of God.

"Fels, you will understand. I've given you a lot today. It will all coalesce in your mind over the next few days and weeks. Just rely on Him in all things. Have faith, hope, and love."

David stood and extended his hand to Fels. With warm smiles on both their faces, they shook hands firmly, and David left the diner.

Fels looked around. The older man was at the cash register counting out his change for the waitress. The two younger men were eating their food. None of them was aware of anything out of the ordinary that may have been taking place. Only minutes had passed since Fels and David talked. Fels sat in wonder. Moments later, the waitress brought Fels a cup of coffee and placed it on the table before him.

That night, Fels lay back in bed and thought about Marie. For the first time, he didn't think about his loss of Marie; rather, he thought about her faith and his faith and about praying together with her. A warmth seemed to appear beside him. He felt the veil being torn away and the fullness of light surrounding him. He didn't understand what was happening to him. It felt as if he was coming back to life, and as if Marie was sitting in the room with him.

For the first time since the day he awoke from his head injury, Fels cried a true heartfelt cry. A few tears rolled down his cheek before he broke down and sobbed into his pillow. "Oh, Marie, how I miss you and the children! I'm sorry I wasn't there for you. I don't understand why God let this happen. God, help me understand. Guide me and strengthen me to do whatever is right in your eyes. I know everything should be handled according to your will. Oh, God, give me strength ...."

Fels then recalled the words David had quoted to him from the Psalms in the hospital: "The Lord is close to the brokenhearted and saves those who are crushed in spirit."

Fels comprehended that the psalmist was discussing those who face adversity not due to their own sinfulness, but because of the presence of trouble in the world. Fels understood that while it is impossible to escape God's presence, it is more than possible to pretend he is not there. That is what Fels had been doing.

Fels was reminded that God is not only present with us, but near. Near to the pain we feel. Near to the loss we are unable fill. Near to the needs we have but cannot express. God gives us the courage we need to breathe again. When we receive His love and the gift of His presence, our hearts are calmed, which frees us to move forward.

Fels eventually cried himself to sleep. But this time, they were tears of joy, a joy he had not known for a very, very long time.

CHAPTER 16

Fels had not yet reported the death of Sporco, and he knew he should do that right away. The entire incident weighed heavily on his mind. He had not told his captain about his investigation, and now Sporco was dead. He went over the pursuit in his head numerous times. His effort to save Sporco was done properly as an officer of the law. In the process, he had almost lost his own life. No, he felt justified in his actions.

But all of this was overshadowed by what David had revealed to him. When he awoke in the morning, he had to wonder if it was all just a dream. He had to check himself to be sure what had taken place was real. His wet clothes were still on the chair where he had left them last night. It was true. He knew he could share nothing about David with the captain, for he would surely think that Fels had lost his mind.

He made himself a light breakfast before leaving for the precinct. Sitting in Captain Flynn's office a half-hour later, Fels provided all the specifics of the prior day's late afternoon activities. He, of course, left out the details about David.

Flynn chastised Fels for pursuing the killer on his own and for not immediately reporting the events to the precinct last night. Flynn knew Fels' penchant for following his instincts and thinking unconventionally. Fels was, in fact, his best detective, not just the best in the precinct, but the best in the entire department. Still, he let Fels know in no uncertain terms that he had not acted appropriately in this situation.

At the same time, Flynn was understanding of Fels' plight. He knew Fels had yet to fully recover from the loss of his family. Yes, his actions were hasty and dangerous, and he did not want Fels to take any undo risks while the events of losing his family still fogged his mind. Flynn stood from his chair behind his desk and stepped over beside Fels.

"Fels, ya know, I just can't let this sorta thing go. Discipline and order must be maintained on the force. You, of anyone, cert'nly understand this." He placed his hand on Fels' shoulder. "Fels, yer gonna have ta take some more time off. I think ya still need some healin'. Maybe not so much physically as gettin' your head around yer situation."

"What situation is that?" Fels challenged.

"Ya know what I'm sayin'. Ya need ta heal from the loss of yer family." He was now squeezing Fels' shoulder.

"Yes, I know what you're saying. It's not a 'situation.' It's the death of my wife, and my son, and my daughter. It's the death of everything I held dear!" Tears welled up in Fels' eyes. He felt like he was saying it out loud to another person for the first time. He grabbed Flynn's arm and broke down.

After several minutes, Fels composed himself. He somehow knew that he had needed to let go as he had. As David had offered him hope by providing an understanding of the heaven where his family now resided, he had now come to terms with his internal loss and had let it all go. The revelations provided by David the night before and this moment with Captain Flynn elevated him to a new sense of direction. He was done with any vengeance. He knew he no longer needed to mourn for his family, and now he knew he no longer needed to mourn for himself. He would move forward with his role as a law enforcement officer and peacekeeper.

Peacekeeper. That was the word David had used. It was that role in law enforcement that he had, as had many others, forgotten. It was the one thing that had made him successful as a young patrol officer. As a peacekeeper, Fels maintained order in the neighborhoods and communities where he served. Peace was achieved by enforcing local laws and ordinances and by working within the neighborhood or community to resolve conflicts. Fels had earned the respect of the people in the neighborhoods by assisting them in resolving their own problems. It was the justice delivered by rescuing people from danger, protecting their physical property from theft and destruction, and reconciling incompatible forms of conduct in public spaces. It was all about developing relationships. This was one way in which Fels helped improve the police perceptions among the general public.

Fels knew he could not explain this epiphany to Flynn, but he was okay with that. Flynn was correct in his assessment of Fels up until the last few moments. Fels was ready, but Flynn was not ready to see that. This was fine with Fels. He could accept his position as Flynn understood it. And now, Fels could do some more investigation to provide a solid case before revealing the bits of the possible plot by the men to place explosives at the powerstations. He would need more than just a few disjointed words overheard through a door. He saw now that he could take his mind off the failure to capture Sporco, and investigating the sabotage plot was just the

thing to focus on. If there truly was some plot being undertaken to destroy the powerstations, it was Fels' duty
to stop the plan ... and keep the peace.

Captain Flynn extended Fels' leave and sent him
home. The extended leave gave Fels the opportunity he
needed to continue his investigation. He made plans to
return to Sporco's apartment and see what he could uncover. He recalled the men had not left the apartment
with the materials they had arrived with, so the evidence
had to be somewhere in Sporco's apartment.

After some effort the following day, Fels was able to
get his motorcycle in running order. It had a few dings
and dents, but it was running just fine. Fels cleaned it
up, brought the engine to life, and mounted the motorcycle. He was heading to Sporco's tenement.

Arriving in Niagara Falls, Fels took the same precau-
tions he had taken on his previous stakeout. He did not
know if the other men might be looking for Sporco as
well. He parked his motorcycle near the same shed as he
had before and walked to the tenement building. Observing every nook and stoop as he went, Fels assured himself that none of the other men were outside watching
the tenement.

As if he were a resident, he approached the building
and entered. He bounded up the stairs to Sporco's floor
and went directly to the door marked 5B. Approaching
the door, he slowed down, stood to one side of the doorway, and leaned in with his ear to the door. After hearing
no movement, Fels rapped quickly and solidly three
times on the door; then he waited, saying nothing. After
a moment, he knocked three times again, this time a little harder and louder. He listened again with his ear to
the door. He heard no sound that might indicate someone was inside.

As before, Fels easily opened the old door lock. He
took his time turning the handle, listening for any activ-

ity inside as he did so. Hearing nothing, he opened the door ever so slightly and waited. He then looked up and down the hall. Seeing no one, Fels slipped into the apartment and closed the door behind him. After rapidly scanning the scene in front of him, Fels locked the door and took a deep breath.

In the center of the room was a wooden table. There were two chairs at the table. One chair was pulled away from the table. In front of that chair on the table was a small bowl with a spoon in it. Next to the bowl was a coffee mug. Approaching the table, Fels noted the bowl contained dried milk, and the mug contained dried coffee. They had obviously not been recently used. There was a small table in the corner, and a third chair was placed in front of it. To the right of the large table was a fireplace. Fels checked the fireplace and noted that it showed no signs of recent use.

Fels approached a doorway to the right. He peered around the corner into the small kitchen area. He would check the kitchen later, and turned around to a corresponding doorway on the opposite wall to the left of the entrance to the main room. There was a dirty curtain pulled to one side. Fels leaned into the doorway and saw two empty beds and two small chests of drawers.

He turned back to the front door. He listened at the door for any activity in the hallway. Hearing nothing, he returned to the bedroom. He looked through the three drawers of each mismatched chest. He found just a few articles of clothing, but nothing of interest. He searched beneath the beds and under each mattress. There was nothing in the stuffy room that proved helpful to him.

Fels crossed back through the main room and entered the kitchen. On the left, he passed the cold stove with a coffee pot on it and approached a set of shelves on the right. There were a few meager pots and a frying pan, a tin of sugar and a tin of flour, three plates, another bowl, and another coffee mug. As with everything else he had inspected, there were no clues to be found. This was a simple, basic, poor tenement apartment.

Fels took two steps to the sink at the far end of the room. A shelf to the right contained some utensils and a small dirty towel on a towel rack. What caught Fels' eye was a mirrored medicine cabinet above the sink. Sitting beneath the cabinet on the sink was a small bar of soap and a shaving mug with a brush in it. Next to the mug was a closed straight razor.

Fels reached out and pulled open the medicine cabinet. Observing closely, he noticed it was not mounted to the wall, but rather it was recessed into the wall. Holding the door halfway open, Fels noticed the cabinet was loose in the wall opening. Fels opened the cabinet door all the way; the cabinet was empty. It did not even contain any shelves.

He examined the condition of the wall cabinet and confirmed that it was indeed loose. Gripping both sides of the cabinet, Fels eased it out of the wall. Resting the cabinet on the sink, he peered inside the void in the wall, certain that he would find something concealed within. He looked up, then down. He could see nothing but the brick and mortar of the exterior wall. He was hopeful he would uncover something secretly hidden. Fels peered downward again as far as he could see into the dark recess. Nothing.

Fels closed the cabinet door and grasped the sides of the cabinet. About to lift the cabinet back into place, he looked down and noticed something on the back of the cabinet. He lifted the cabinet and turned it around. Taped securely to the back of the cabinet was a large envelope. Fels lifted the flap of the envelope, glanced inside, and noticed many folded papers.

He reached his hand inside the envelope and retrieved the bundle of papers. Fels took the contents of the envelope and walked to the small table in the main room of the apartment. In his hands were single sheets, a slim bound notebook, and three larger folded papers.

Fels went through the single sheets one at a time. Each was a carefully printed message of sorts. There was confirmation of arrivals of certain individuals. He saw four names: Peter Niemand, Robert Werner, Otto Bergman, and ... Paul Sporco. He did not recognize the first three names, but they were now tied to Sporco.

Another set of papers confirmed addresses and meeting locations. Other pages appeared more cryptic, perhaps coded in some manner, but talked of plans to commence with the project. This part puzzled Fels. *What project?*

Fels retrieved a notebook and pencil from his coat pocket and began making notes of names, places, and times. He noted the addresses of the "project" sites. He would confirm the addresses later, but they seemed oddly familiar to him.

Fels next honed in on the folded papers. It shocked him to see drawings showing the location of three large turbines at a powerstation in Niagara Falls. Entrances and exits were clearly marked, and there was an indication of a pathway to each turbine. The turbines were marked on the drawing with numbers 2, 6, and 8 circled. There was another drawing for another powerstation with turbine number 2 marked. It then hit him that the locations of the powerstations were the addresses of the project.

Fels dove back into the loose papers and the bound pages that seemed to be a key to the coded messages. While unable to uncover a timeline of probable events, Fels did uncover a completion date for the project, November 24. This was the day before the Day of Thanksgiving, as declared by President Wilson on October 20.

The "celebration" was to take place at 7:00 a.m. on that day. It was becoming clear in Fels' mind.

"My God!" Fels found himself speaking out loud. It was at that moment that Fels heard a knock on the door. Fels returned to the kitchen and quickly placed the contents back in the envelope. There was another knock on the door as he replaced the cabinet in the wall.

A third knock and, "C'mon, Paul, open up. We need to talk."

Fels approached the window in the main room. He lifted it slowly.

"Look, Paul," the voice whispered through the door, "we think they may be on to us." Then, the voice grew louder with more concern."We have to talk now! Open up!" There was more banging on the door.

Fels exited the window to the fire escape and closed it behind him.

He could still hear the voices that grew louder. "Paul, open up or we'll have to break this door down. We have to talk now!"

Fels stood to the side of the window on the fire escape. Inside, the door flew open and two men stumbled in. With only a quick glance, Fels recognized the faces. It was the two men who had been at Sporco's on Fels' previous visit, the men he followed to the tavern, the men who met the older man at Shorty's tavern.

The men entered the bedroom in search of Sporco, and Fels made his way down the fire escape.

CHAPTER 17

Fels knew that he could not sit on the information he had uncovered. While he had none of the actual papers to prove what he had found, his notes provided very detailed information that should be enough to get the attention of the BOI through Agent Blackmon. Fels returned to his apartment, where he organized his notes and added every piece of information that he could recall.

When he was confident with his unofficial report of what he had uncovered, Fels called Blackmon and arranged a meeting for that evening. Over dinner, Fels shared his notes with Blackmon and provided all the minutest of detail he could remember. Blackmon listened intently. He did not interrupt Fels with any questions as he gave his clear and concise report. However, when Fels had completed his statement, Blackmon tossed question after question at Fels and added to his own exhaustive set of interview notes.

Fels finished speaking, sighed, and looked up at Blackmon. He felt as if he had unburdened himself of some weight. One thing that still troubled Fels, however, was that he had only looked at two of the three drawings of the powerstation locations that were the obvious targets. What else was there that was missing?

"Myron, we have to act on this ... and soon. I'm really bothered that I was unable to look at what was likely a third drawing of another set of powerstations." He looked to Blackmon for confirmation of the next steps. A high degree of trust in Blackmon had developed in Fels.

Blackmon gathered his thoughts and then spoke. "Fels, this is a very serious manner. You've done good work in getting the information that you have. Unfortunately, this is not a BOI matter." He winced as he finished the sentence, for he knew how Fels would react. He waited for a response, which came quickly.

"What do you mean?! Myron, this is a planned attack on the powerstations by the Germans!"

"That's exactly why I can't proceed with this. This is clearly something that must be turned over to the Secret Service. They must be brought in on anything to do with Germany and the war. They are very clear about this, and so is my director. No, Fels, this must be taken to the Secret Service."

"Okay, but we need to do this now. It appears to me that this is planned to take place the day before the president's declared Day of Thanksgiving for this year. Myron, that's only about four weeks away!"

"I understand your concern for urgency. I'll contact the Secret Service and arrange a meeting with them just as soon as we can. Can you have your notes typed up for a meeting with them?"

"Sure. I'll have to bring Captain Flynn in on this in order to do that."

Making Captain Flynn aware of his activities would take some careful explaining for sure, but Fels knew what the alternative meant. He would likely be berated by Flynn for acting on his own ... again. There was no alternative, however, whatever the personal consequences might be for Fels.

"That's fine. I'll call you as soon as I have the meeting set up."

Three days later, at the 5th Precinct, Fels, Blackmon, and Captain Flynn met with Special Agent of the Secret Service, Henry Wilson. Fels had arrived early to check Flynn's temperature after he had a few days to think about Fels' actions. Only the gravity of the situation had kept Captain Flynn from immediately dismissing Fels. It wasn't often that Captain Flynn raised his voice, but Fels had heard him loud and clear. Flynn's temperament had only slightly moderated since Fels had informed him of the plot against the powerstations.

The four men representing their different law enforcement organizations met behind closed doors in Captain Flynn's office. Special Agent Wilson of the Secret Service was the first to arrive shortly after Fels met with Captain Flynn. He was a short man with a small mustache. He was very well-dressed, wore a bow tie, and sported a bowler hat of the finest quality. His suit looked as if it had just come off the rack at the finest men's clothier. The agent's small stature was outweighed by his large personality. In no uncertain terms, Agent Wilson immediately took charge of the meeting.

"So, I understand you have some information that may be of importance to the Secret Service. Agent Blackmon briefly explained the situation to me, but Detective Krieger, I understand you have prepared your notes from an investigation. Could you share those?"

Fels picked up the typed pages of his notes and handed them to Agent Wilson. Wilson scanned the papers, shuffling the pages back and forth as he did so. His stern expression was unchanging during his study of Fels' report. He gleaned the information as if preparing for an interrogation. He took his time, and occasionally verbalized his review with a simple, "Hmm."

"Now, Detective Krieger, do you have in your possession any of the documents you referenced in your report?"

"No. As I noted, I was interrupted in the apartment and felt it best to replace the documents before leaving. I thought—"

"Yes, I see. You, then, have no actual evidence to support your allegations." Agent Wilson was firm and to the point. He did not wait for Fels to reply, "No, you do not. This appears to me to be a bit sloppy, as far as an investigation is concerned." He looked at the papers in his hand, and then lowered them to his side. "Am I to understand that you were actually supposed to be on leave at the time of your 'investigation'?"

"I—"

"Again, no need to reply. I already know the answer."

As Fels' face reddened, Blackmon jumped in, "Agent Wilson, if I may. There were some extenuating circumstances involving the detective's investigation. I can personally vouch for his skills in his investigative work. I—"

"Fine, Detective Krieger is good at his job, and you are a finely trained BOI agent ... whose expertise is in accounting, as I understand it." He lifted his eyebrows as he trained his gaze on Blackmon. He had done his due diligence on the backgrounds of both men.

Agent Wilson handed the report back to Fels. "Thank you, gentlemen, for your efforts, but with all due respect, this is a matter for the Secret Service. And, I might add, you are late to the party. You see, we are already aware of these plots to destroy the locks and the powerstations.

"This all started with a plot to blow up the locks at the Welland Canal in order to cripple a potentially vital supply line to Great Britain. Gentlemen, what I am about to share with you cannot leave this room. I trust you understand this, and I have your agreement?" His eyes moved from man to man, stopping for a split second at each.

All heads nodded.

"There are numerous plots that have been planned against the United States to discourage us from providing any assistance to Great Britain in this conflict with Germany. We've been able to deduce that the German intelligence organization known simply as Section 3-B is responsible for implementing these plots These plots are all being coordinated by the German Ambassador to the United States, Johann von Bernstorff.

"Now, several plots are under the direct control of German Military Attache Franz von Papen, who has recruited the men to carry out these bombings."

Agent Wilson paused and again looked each man directly in the eyes. His tone was both somber and proud. "Again, none of this leaves this room, but I am comfortable sharing this with you as we will announce shortly our arrests of several suspects in these plots. We have already stopped the plot to destroy the locks at the Welland Canal, and we will also shortly announce arrests in conjunction with the Canadian authorities on plots involving the destruction of the powerstations."

He once again paused, this time merely for effect. "So, as you can see, the Secret Service is way ahead of you on this. But, as always, we appreciate the vigilant efforts of local law enforcement, and, of course, of the BOI." Agent Wilson exposed a proud smile as he lifted his small stature as tall as he could. His condescending tone was obviously purposeful in nature.

Fels spoke up, "Agent Wilson, you mentioned the Welland Canal, and you mentioned the Canadian authorities regarding the powerstations. From the information I was able to gather, there was no mention of American powerstations—"

"Thank you, detective, but we have the entire expanse of these plots under control. You do not need to concern yourself with any further efforts toward this case. We have the situation contained, and arrests will be forthcoming." There was no longer a hint of a smile on the agent's face as he stroked his mustache.

"But does that include the American powerstations? Is the name Paul Sporco included on your list for those arrests? I—"

Agent Wilson lost whatever patience he might have had. "Look, Detective Krieger, we have everyone accounted for. While there was nothing specific regarding the turbines at the powerstations which you noted in your report, we believe we have put an end to the plot." He paused to be sure Fels heard him. "Besides, you saw your man go over the falls. That's about as final as you can get for this Mr. Sporco."

"But, Agent Wilson, there were at least three other German men involved. Paul Sporco was only one of them. If you don't have them, then they are still out there!"

"Calm down, Detective Krieger! We have everyone accounted for. Do you have other names for me besides those in your report?"

"No, but Sporco was working with these other men, and he specifically referred to the powerstations."

"Look, Krieger, unless you have something more than the supposition of a dead man, I suggest you take comfort in the fact that Mr. Sporco received God's justice, and you move on with getting your life back together." He was now completely focused on Fels, his voice rising with each word.

Frustrated, Fels slammed his fist on Captain Flynn's desk. "You aren't hearing me!"

Agent Wilson stepped forward, so he was nose to nose with Fels. "I think it's time for you to leave, detective! If we uncover anything else for which we might need your assistance, we'll call your office. Now, back off!"

Agent Wilson glared at Fels. Fels glared back. After a silent moment, Fels grabbed his hat and left the office, muttering unintelligibly under his breath, "Am I wrong?"

After the meeting had broken up, Fels returned to Captain Flynn's office. Fels pleaded his case to the captain. But his balloon had been deflated by Agent Wilson. He had lost some portion of credibility with Captain Flynn at this point.

"Fels, if ya felt strongly about this, ya would've pursued it earlier. I know yer instincts. Yer first intuition has always been right. In this case, it was somethin' ya told me in passin'. We brought it ta the Secret Service, and they took over. If they say they've wrapped it up, then let it go. Besides, Agent Wilson shared with me that the individuals in this case have used several aliases. He said any additional names are simply aliases of individuals that they've already identified."

Fels knew the real reason he had not pushed the issue —he was focused on finding his family's killer. Nothing else really mattered to him at the time. He had set aside his suspicions and instead organized all his thoughts and actions to finding the killer.

But now he realized that there was something bigger at stake. He now knew that his actual intuition had been correct. He ignored it to pursue his family's killer. It was time to get to the bottom of this. Yes, he'd take his time off. If there was a plot to blow up the powerstations, and if it was still active, he would uncover it.

CHAPTER 18

The Tonawanda Police Department announced the death of the killer of Fels' family, closing the case. It was made very clear that this was not a mob hit, but rather it was the action of a lone killer. The police gave little attention to the circumstances of the killer's demise. The report simply noted that the killer, Paul Sporco, had died at Niagara Falls after a police pursuit. Fels was pleased that they had reported it in this manner. He did not want to explain the events of Sporco's death to anyone outside of his superiors, although it seemed many of the patrol officers knew the complete story. And certainly all of them would know the details of the encounter in a short time. Fels received veiled forms of congratulations for his handling of the case from many of the men.

After general interest in the situation simmered, despite understanding Fels' situation in this case, the department gave him an official reprimand and extended his leave without pay for another four weeks. Captain Flynn had noted to Chief Bruckhart that he had already given Fels additional leave. But Chief Bruckhart felt that for the good of the department and the community, it would be best for an appended reprimand. While the report to the newspaper did not release any of this information, it gained prominent attention once the details of Sporco's death were exposed through the rumor mill.

The community had a mixed reaction to the news. All were glad that the killer had been found. And most everyone had some degree of sympathy for Detective Krieger. But, at the same time, many felt that Fels had acted outside the law in his pursuit. There were even some who were convinced Fels had purposely let Sporco drown by denying him help. So, he accepted his official reprimand, and in the end, this action brought closure to the matter.

Fels retraced all of his steps in his pursuit of Sporco. He needed to satisfy himself that he had handled everything properly. While he accepted his additional reprimand, he needed to know for certain that his state of mind had not tainted his actions. He was fully aware he had gone too far with the questioning of Mosher, and his actions weighed heavily upon him. That issue was now between him and God. He had to be sure he had not made the same mistake with his pursuit of Sporco.

Sporco had recognized Fels, and there was no other reason for him to know Fels' identity other than as the killer of his family. Fels recalled the look in Sporco's eyes. He had recognized Fels, and he knew he was in big trouble. Everything in Sporco's actions told Fels that this was the murderer of his family. There was absolutely no doubt in Fels' mind. When Sporco ran, Fels had to pursue him; it would have been derelict of him not to do so.

The rain proved to be a factor that affected the pursuit significantly. If Fels had not had his motorcycle, he would have lost Sporco for sure. But then, it was David's help in directing him in Sporco's direction near the bridge that let him gain on Sporco in the chase. If David was helping him, then Fels certainly had to be doing the right thing. There would have been no other reason for David's presence at that time.

Of course, what it came down to was Sporco's life having been lost in the river. Had Fels purposely allowed Sporco to be pulled to his death in the raging waters and carried over the falls? Fels played it all out in his mind, over and over. *No! I jumped into the rapids myself, attempting to save Sporco! I wanted him to live, to stand trial for his actions, to receive the justice he deserved. As much as I had previously wanted vengeance, at that moment, I wanted to save the man. I almost drowned in the process myself. In fact, I would have drowned had it not been for David.*

Fels knew he had done the right thing. He also knew that David had saved him to fulfill his purpose in life. Despite his lingering uncertainty, one thing was becoming clear to him—he had a job to do as an officer of the law, and as a peacekeeper. He knew in his heart that right now the job was to find out if this plot to blow the powerstations was real or not. And, if it was real, then it meant Fels must stop it and save the lives of good people. Officially on the force or not, Fels must continue his investigation and stop the saboteurs.

A few days after the closing of the Sporco case, all the local newspapers carried a headlined story about the plot by the Germans to blow up the Welland Canal. Fels had been anticipating the announcement from the Secret Service. He wanted to see how broad the plot was, as recorded in the report from the Secret Service. He wanted some assurance that the plot to blow up the powerstations was truly stopped as a part of the larger plan. He wanted that assurance because his very core told him that the American powerstations were still in play for the Germans.

Stopping at a newsstand near his apartment, Fels scanned a few of the newspaper headlines, "Germans Arrested at N.Y. Charged with Conspiracy to Blow up Welland Canal," then, "Enemy Plot to Destroy Welland Canal Discovered in New York; Two Arrested," and, "Hun Plot to Destroy Welland Canal Nipped in Bud at New York." He mulled over the first few lines of each story and pulled one of the newspapers to scan the front-page article.

"New York, October 28, 1915 — A plot to blow up the Welland Canal is charged in connection with the arrest recently of three prominent Germans. The arrests are said to be the prelude to a series of startling exposures of German propaganda in this country, which may link together a number of events that have occurred in the United States.

"The first man arrested was Paul Koenig, police superintendent of the Hamburg-German American Line, and believed to be the head of the German secret service in America."

Fels skipped ahead. "The second man is Richard Emil Leyendecker, retailer of art goods living in the Bronx. He is a naturalized American citizen, and these arrests make the first instance where the so-called 'hyphenated Americans' have been arrested in connection with German propaganda.

"The third person arrested was Fred Metzler, alias F. R. Reimer, who was arrested in Jersey City."

Only three arrested?! Where are the rest? Fels scanned quickly through the rest of the article, "These men are charged with Section 13 of the Federal Criminal Statutes with planning a military undertaking of hazard against a country friendly with the United States ...

"The precise details of the alleged plot were withheld by the Federal authorities, but it is understood that Koenig and Leyendecker had employed spies, who went out from Buffalo and Niagara Falls to photograph the canal, prepare plans, and make arrangements for blowing up the waterway at its most important point ...

"They packed up a great mass of material concerning the movements of German secret agents. Secret codes, which were changed every week to elude any persons who might have been shadowing them, or listening over telephones, also were found.

"... in addition to these codes, there were found many other documents of great importance, over which the detectives and agents are pouring, including maps and drawings of the Welland Canal."

The article contained a bit of the story of the canal itself. "Before the Welland Canal's construction, cargo was transported overland between Chippewa and Queenston on the Niagara River. In 1824, the province of Upper Canada allowed for the formation of the Welland Canal Company for the canal's construction. The first Welland Canal's construction began in November 1824 and opened five years later, in November 1829. The canal opened a lifeline of trade and commerce to inland North America. In 1841, the canal company began deepening the existing canal, completing what is known as the second Welland Canal in 1854. Presently, construction started in 1913 on the third Welland Canal."

Further down, "A previous attempt by saboteurs to destroy the canal was made the evening of April 21, 1900, when a dynamite charge was set off against the hinges of Lock No. 24. The blast only resulted in minor damage."

Fels scanned the rest of the news report, but saw nothing regarding any plot to blow up the powerstations on the Niagara River. He grabbed another newspaper and quickly scanned it. The report was basically the same with a few more details on Paul Koenig, as well as more details on the actual charges against the three men. But, again, there was nothing about the powerstations.

Fels closed the newspaper. *Are those arrests yet to come? Are they maybe gathering more materials for evidence? No, Agent Wilson said they had everything, including the powerstation plot.*

Fels decided he would wait a few days to see if there were any more reports about the plot to blow up the powerstations. He stopped by the newsstand each morning and afternoon to check the newspapers. On the second day, a report appeared. It noted that, in further conjunction with Canadian authorities, arrests had been made regarding a German plot associated with the Welland Canal plot. This plot was to blow up three Canadian powerstations along the Niagara River. The article went on to say that the combined efforts of the agents of the two countries had not only ended the German destructive efforts in the U.S., but had also exposed a spy ring that had penetrated the country from coast to coast. It was only a matter of time before additional plots were exposed and more arrests would be made. It also referred to numerous aliases used by those involved.

Fels pondered how he could approach Agent Wilson to ask about the plot to blow up the American powerstations. He wanted to ask about the aliases to see if any matched the names he had uncovered. But most importantly, *Had the plot against the American powerstations been exposed and stopped?* Fels knew he could not ask Agent Wilson, nor could he ask BOI Agent Blackmon to contact Agent Wilson.

No, Fels made up his mind to continue his investigation to be sure that this plot was foiled. There was that detective instinct that kept pestering him not to back off. *Surely, the plot to destroy the powerstations will take place unless I intervene. I just don't feel that Agent Wilson is aware of this specific plot. I've got to get the evidence to convince him.* He hoped he could still count on Blackmon for help if needed.

CHAPTER 19

With growing concern and frustration, Fels thought a good workout at Turners might help clear his head. It bothered him very much that he had no credibility with Agent Wilson. He thought the agent was full of himself and too quick to dismiss others, but still he had hoped for more respect from him. Captain Flynn was now harboring doubts about his fitness to perform his duties. He was even let down by Chief Bruckhart when he placed him on additional leave. However, he was certain that his credibility with the chief had not been compromised. While it still felt a little like the rug being pulled out from under him, he understood what the chief had to do. He fully trusted his instincts, and he had proven himself in the past, but it seemed as if that had all been washed away.

He pushed his well-toned body hard at Turners. It felt good to work his muscles to the point of exhaustion. The sweat poured through his pores as if it was purging his troubles. He felt the harder he pushed himself, the more likely he was to gain a sense of direction. The exertion he placed on his body freed his mind to allow fresh ideas to flow. But, it was nothing but dead ends ... except for Blackmon.

Blackmon was the only one who trusted in what Fels had heard and seen. Blackmon had the best understanding of the circumstances. It was Blackmon, more than the captain or the chief with whom he had worked closely with for years, who trusted Fels and came to his defense against Agent Wilson. Fels sensed Blackmon was feeling the same disappointment that he had felt in their treatment by Wilson at the meeting. Agent Wilson had basically looked at the BOI Agent as a simple accountant, giving no credibility to his ongoing role in bringing down organized crime in Western New York. Blackmon must have felt stung by the disrespect from Agent Wilson as well. Yes, Agent Blackmon was Fels' only resource at this time.

But now he would certainly be asking Blackmon to put his job on the line. Agent Wilson had made it clear that both men were to fully disengage from any investigative activity into the matter. Blackmon was doubtless at a greater risk from a much higher level of authority. He had made a good career for himself through diligent work, and Fels loathed the thought that he could be responsible for taking down the man's career. And besides, Blackmon had a family to support, something that was no longer a point in question for Fels. Fels felt as though he had inadvertently stabbed himself as that thought pierced his mind. *But, it's true. I have nothing to lose. Can I ask Blackmon to risk so much?*

Fels thought about his own career. The career itself was no longer the important issue to Fels. He knew he had to see this through, no matter the cost to himself. This was so much larger than his career in law enforcement. This single act of espionage could wreak havoc on America's abilities to support Great Britain in their war with Germany. It could be a true turning point as the events played out.

Of course, there was David. But what would he ask of David? No, he had a better understanding of David's role in his life. David's province was not to be there to make every decision for Fels or to move every roadblock out of his way. David had helped Fels get his life back in order with an understanding of his own spirit. David had enabled Fels to get on that path to the purpose of his life. He did not know when, or even if, he would see David again. No, he couldn't just call on David like a magic genie. That was clear. That very thought was actually abhorrent to Fels. David had brought Fels back to life, and Fels could expect nothing more.

With a renewed sense of urgency, Fels reached out to Blackmon. He felt guilty about asking the man to help him out one more time, and this time could have even greater repercussions.

It was Saturday, and Fels just couldn't wait until Monday, so he phoned Blackmon at home and asked if they could meet for supper. He heard Blackmon explain to his wife that he had to go to work. Fels was now sorry that he had put him in that position. Fels apologized, but Blackmon told him that was unnecessary. He would meet him for supper.

As they waited for their meal, Blackmon shared some news with Fels. "Fortunately for me, Agent Wilson informed the BOI Special Agent in Charge in New York that I had been read in on the plots and that the Secret Service appreciated I had properly turned over to them what we had uncovered. I was also told to watch my involvement with local law enforcement, especially regarding you specifically. Apparently, Agent Wilson has not done you any favors."

Fels rolled his eyes at the last comment. "Well, Agent Wilson is too dull to understand what we handed to him on a silver platter. I'm glad that he didn't put you in a compromising position, Myron. Believe me, I don't want to be responsible for any backlash on you because of my relationship with Agent Wilson."

Blackmon felt Fels needed to get to the point. "I'd like to say that this is all behind us, Fels, but I have a feeling that you are not backing off."

"You're right about that. I've thought long and hard about this. Look, everything we've uncovered is specific to an attack on the American powerstations. There's nothing at all telling me that what we found involves the Canadian side. Do you agree?"

"I understand what you're saying, but that doesn't totally rule out a connection. They could be two separate teams working on one overarching plan. It would make sense to have a team on each side of the river. If so, then Agent Wilson may be correct when he says they have stopped it all."

Fels countered, "Or, they could be two separate teams working on two separate, but related, plans. Think about it. In the scenario where two teams are unaware of each other, if one team gets exposed, the other team can still carry out a portion of the mission. Even taking out only the Canadian or only the American side would be devastating. It would certainly improve any chance of success of the overall goal of the Germans."

"I'm trying to play devil's advocate a bit, but I have to agree with your assessment. As Agent Wilson told us, this goes back to Germany's Section 3-B. This war effort by Germany is a big deal for them. Keeping the Americans out of any type of support to Great Britain is huge. With our involvement, things would be much more difficult for Germany. My gut agrees with you on this, Fels. Pragmatically, it just makes more sense to plan this attack as you outlined."

"The clock is ticking, and we need more information. We can't go back to Agent Wilson without hard evidence. If we don't get something concrete, then we may as well not have anything."

Blackmon agreed. "He'd toss us both out, and we'd both lose our jobs."

Fels stopped and looked directly into Blackmon's eyes. "I'm sorry. I used 'we' when I have not even asked you about being involved in this any further. I'm resigned to the fact that I could lose my job with the Tonawanda PD, and I would likely be unable to get a job in any law enforcement position anywhere in Western New York. But I simply cannot presume that you would want to put your position in any further jeopardy. It would be totally unfair of me to ask this of you—"

Blackmon smiled. "Fels, I'm all in. I'm making my own decision on this. This situation is too big to ignore. As an employee of the federal government, I cannot disregard this when we have as much information as we do, no matter what Agent Wilson threatens. We need to tie up the loose ends and stop this plot!"

Fels leaned back in his chair with a sense of relief. "Then, we have to do this on our own." Fels paused as the wheels turned in his head. His eyes lit up. "Of course! Shorty's Tavern! It's where I followed the two men who had been at Sporco's apartment, where they met with a third man. They were all speaking German. It's what prompted me to return and search Sporco's tenement."

"What is it you want to do?"

Visualizing the plan in his head energized Fels. "I want to go back there and see if any of those men return. Maybe it's a meeting place. I don't see any other options. We don't have a lot of time on this. November 24 will be here before we know it. Myron, I see this as our only play."

Myron pondered momentarily. He knew Fels was right. "Okay, but you have to be careful. You can't arouse any suspicions. If you move too quickly, you could lose any chance of gleaning more information. It's a fine line between gathering useful information and pushing too hard. There's no room for error."

"I know. Look, it was in the late afternoon when the men met. I'll start becoming a regular at the tavern come Monday!"

"You're not going alone." Myron felt Fels seemed a bit too eager. He was concerned that he might move with disregard for his personal safety, which in turn could ruin any hope of getting the information they needed.

"No, I have to." Fels' tone abruptly changed. He pleaded his case with a sense of duty. He was not throwing caution to the wind. "I hear you, but I don't see any way to get you into this thing with Max. I don't think we have enough time, and I'm not even sure, at this point, that we could bring in another new face."

Blackmon saw Fels' commitment in his voice and in his body. He thought for a moment. "Look, Fels, I'll be your back-up on this. You know, I don't have any agents available to offer support, and I couldn't ask them if I did. But you need to have your back covered. I need to be ready to move in if things go sideways. I'll stay at a distance outside just in case anything goes wrong."

"Okay, but get rid of the suit. You'll stick out like a sore thumb."

Blackmon grabbed the lapels of his suit coat. "What, give up my Adler Brothers standard issue suit and starched collar!" Both men laughed, something neither had done for some time. They were both now more relaxed, since they had agreed to continue the investigation. The difficult work was ahead, but their mutual commitment removed all doubt about proceeding.

Through supper and into the evening, the two men discussed how Fels would approach the man at the tavern. They played out different scenarios to ensure Fels would not be caught off-guard in any situation. A backstory was laid out that would make Fels an attractive resource for the plan.

"I'll tell Max I work at the Niagara Power Company. I'll let him know I handle mechanical issues." Fels paused. "I'll let him think I'm a disgruntled German upset with being outcast because of the pending war in Europe. Myron, I can make myself look very appealing to him for what we both know his plans are. You know he needs the help with Sporco out of the picture.

"Assuming he needs to add another member to his cabal, I think I'm in a good position to be drawn in. Further assuming that he invites me in, I'll need to get his last name. Then you can check your BOI records to see if you have anything on him. From there, I hope to confirm the timeline and locations. That should substantiate the information I gathered from Sporco's tenement."

While Fels would not be able to convince anyone of his ability to take the place of Sporco regarding bomb making, perhaps a convincing background in maintenance work at a powerstation would garner their interest. Blackmon told Fels to keep as much of his backstory as possible based on his actual personal story. That would make it much easier to avoid any contradictions if he were to be thoroughly questioned. Lies were easiest sold when they were closest to the truth.

The explosives issue was a genuine concern. If Sporco had not completed his work on the explosives, then they would need someone with that expertise. There was simply no way Fels could be prepared to take Sporco's place in that regard. But, if the bombs were already completed, then it was more a matter of hands and feet to carry out the plan. With the backstory firmed up by the two men,

Fels could be seen as a potential asset to the scheme. Fels would need to sell himself without pushing too hard. A bit of finesse and a lot of luck would be required.

CHAPTER 20

Fels returned to Shorty's Tavern two days later, on Monday. He decided he would become a regular late afternoon customer. He ordered a beer and sat quietly, observing the comings and goings. He had few conversations with the bartender, appearing to be only interested in enjoying a couple of beers after a hard day's work. After three days, he had seen nothing unusual and was concerned that maybe this location had only been used one time for a meeting. Perhaps they were meeting at various locations to avoid arousal of suspicion from anyone. While he was somewhat discouraged, Fels knew that patience was the key to any investigation. Only in this case, he felt time was critical.

Blackmon had been outside and across the street while Fels was in the tavern. From his position near a window in a small coffee shop, Blackmon had a direct view of the front door of the tavern. He also had a full view of the front windows, but they did not allow him to see any detail of activity in the darkened tavern. Blackmon casually sipped his coffee while giving full attention to anything that did not look right at the tavern.

When Fels left the tavern and headed south, Blackmon waited five minutes before leaving the coffee shop. The two men met later, and Fels filled Blackmon in on the lack of activity regarding the older man or either of the men who had been at Sporco's apartment. On the third evening, Blackmon let Fels know that the following evening would have to be canceled. Blackmon had a meeting that he was required to attend. He was adamant that Fels not go alone. Fels was equally adamant that he had to go to the tavern. The two parted that evening with each thinking he had convinced the other of his point of view.

The following day toward suppertime, with no backup at the coffee shop across the street, Fels sat at the bar drinking a beer and finishing a sandwich. From a single door at the back of the room, the heavyset man entered the tavern. He sat at the same table in the rear by the fireplace. Fels noticed he was wearing glasses and carrying a newspaper. As the man sat and raised the newspaper, Fels could just make out the headlines in German. Since few German newspapers were in circulation now with the rumors of war being initiated by Germany, Fels deemed it odd to see the man reading one. It was not something an American would want to be seen doing, and the bar did not seem to provide a discrete location to cover such an act. No, the man seemed openly obvious about it, with little care that anyone should notice.

After placing the last bite of his sandwich in his mouth, Fels paid for his meal and beer, and slowly made his way to the fireplace, which contained a generous fire to chase away the chill in the air. As Fels arrived, the man's eyes peered over the newspaper and above his glasses at Fels. Fels nodded his head and provided a polite smile. The man lowered his eyes back to the newspaper in his hands. The man was not wearing a hat this time, and Fels noted his few strands of brown hair combed straight back over his head. In his best German, Fels asked the man about the situation in Germany and commented that he hadn't seen many German newspapers these days.

The man glanced up over his newspaper again. He stared at Fels as if evaluating whether he was worthy of a reply. The man laughed in a belittling manner. "And just how good is your German, young man?" He lowered the newspaper and haughtily waited for a reply.

In his best German, Fels replied, "Nun, mein vater hat dafür gesorgt, dass wir jungen zu hause nur Deutsch sprachen." Fels paused and smiled again. "My German is just fine," he said in English.

"And I see your English is 'just fine' as well," the man replied directly as he took in a deep breath. The man continued holding the open newspaper.

Fels placed his palms toward the fire, then rubbed his hands together to warm them. "Yes, that was my mother's doing. She saw to it that we all did our best to fit in." Fels laughed. "As if that really mattered. Look how they're treating those of us of German heritage with the impending war."

Fels raised his voice slightly, as if he was growing angry. "I've been called a barbarian and a Hun by people I've worked with for years, by people in my own neighborhood." Fels paused, watching the man's interest grow, before continuing. "Someone slipped a paper under my door. It said, 'Go back to Germany, Kaiser lover!' I'm sick of it!" Fels looked around as if startled that he had spoken so loudly.

The man at the table had a frown on his face. "Sit, my boy." The man folded his newspaper, set it on the table, and motioned to the chair directly across from him. "You are full of spunk now, aren't you?" The man's frown had turned to a smile. He once again drew in a deep, wheezing breath.

Fels pulled out the chair and sat down. "My apologies, sir, if I've upset you."

"On the contrary. I admire such grit in a young man. I, in fact, share your sentiments. Merely speaking the language of our homeland arouses suspicion these days. If we do so, it must be in whispers. Such a shame it is. Our language has a poetic beauty that is simply not found in the English language. Wouldn't you agree?" He was out of breath as he finished speaking and breathed in deeply.

"Of course." Fels could see that the man enjoyed talking about Germany. His eyes reached out to the man as if to say, "Tell me more."

"I have a source for German newspapers!" The man gloated as he slid the folded paper across the table to Fels. "Here, take this one. You can catch up on the news and answer your own question about the situation in Germany."

"Thank you very much. I am humbled." Fels placed the newspaper under his left hand on the table.

"You seem like an intelligent young man. I read people very well, and I can tell you are a man with a strong backbone and a sense of purpose. Am I correct?" The man paused and wiped his brow with his handkerchief before wheezing.

Fels wanted to feed the man's sense of keen perception, but he had to be cautious of overselling his flattery. "Well, I've never thought about it much, but I would say that's accurate. I suppose that's what my mother meant when she said I was stubborn." Both men laughed.

"What's your name, young man?"

Fels extended his hand across the table. With a firm handshake, he replied, "I'm Wilhelm Roloff." He had decided to use his great-grandfather's surname. At least if questioned, he could use his actual family's story to fill in any necessary blanks for the man. "Most people call me Wil."

"Wil, I am Maximilian. You, of course, may call me Max, as my close associates do."

Close associates? So far, so good, Fels thought. "Thank you, Max ... uh, do you have a last name?" Fels hoped he wasn't pushing too hard, but he needed the man's name.

The man stared into Fels' eyes. He continued the grip of Fels' hand and tightened it. Fels felt as though Max was going to pull him across the table. "In due time, Wil, in due time." He let loose of Fels' hand, but he continued looking deeply into Fels' eyes. Fels did not back down. "First, tell me more about yourself. What sort of work are you in? What skills do you possess?" Max relaxed back in his chair.

Fels had already prepared a backstory, one he hoped would intrigue the man. "I work at the Niagara Power Company." Fels watched Max's face closely, noticing the slight upturn in his eyebrows. He had Max's attention. "I'm pretty good at taking care of mechanical problems. I'm not an engineer or anything, but I maintain a lot of the more common equipment. I've worked there for about five years now."

Fels paused and saw the continued interest in Max's eyes; however, he stopped at this point with information about his supposed current job at the power plant. He wanted to arouse Max's interest, but he did not want it to appear as though he was pushing the fact upon Max. He hoped to have Max himself ask for the details. He watched as Max's large stomach rose and fell with each labored breath.

"Before that, I had a small repair shop. Mostly mechanical stuff, bicycles, wagons, farm equipment. Like I said, I have a good mechanical aptitude. I still do a little repair work. Of course, with the current situation, that business has all but dried up."

Fels feigned a rising anger in his tone. "I'm sure my skills would be highly valued in the German homeland." Fels paused to call up some more anger. He sat up very straight in his chair. "You know what, Max? I'm spending more and more of my time at the power plant sitting in the stock room! My boss and my non-German co-workers seem to want to see less of me out in the plant! I'm just sick of it!" Fels ended with a heavy, loud sigh.

Fels was about to drop his fist to the table but stopped short of the tabletop. While he wanted Max to see his anger, he also wanted Max to see that he had control. As he stopped his arm, he looked meekly about the room. "My apologies, Max. I shouldn't have acted like that in front of you." Fels lowered his head slightly and used his eyes to show false shame and submission to Max.

Max sat forward in his chair. "No apologies necessary, my boy. I understand your frustration, perhaps better than you realize."

"Thank you for that kindness." Fels lowered his eyes.

After a pause in which Max seemed to mull over his evaluation of Fels, Max inquired more deeply. "Tell me about the plant where you work. Is that the one where the underground tunnel begins? Is that something one could actually visit?" His manner remained serious, and Fels detected a rise in his interest.

"Yes, that's the plant where the tunnel begins. There's a small inlet canal that brings the water from the Niagara River into the powerstation houses." Fels continued to provide the information he had been able to glean with Blackmon's help. "It's really something to see. The water surges down to the pit wheels below the powerhouse in immense torrents. They produce electricity when the spinning turbines rotate the massive generators."

The discussion continued, and Fels shared nearly every fact he had memorized. From 1892 to 1894, the Niagara Falls Power Company built the 6,700-foot long, 21-foot high, and 18-foot wide horseshoe shaped tunnel which is 160 feet underground. The water falls down the vertical shaft to the tunnel, providing the power to spin the turbines. Fels shared a bit of the history he had learned. Twenty-eight workers died in construction related accidents during the construction. Extending from the Niagara Power Company Powerhouse underground and exiting back into the river below the falls, the tunnel displaced 300,000 tons of rock and required 20 million bricks to complete.

"There's a maintenance shaft down to the tunnel. The full hundred and sixty feet! I've been down there many times for routine safety checks. It was a little scary at first, but I've gotten used to it. It's sure not for the faint of heart!" Fels displayed an excitement in talking about the workings of the powerstations.

Fels had been careful not to make himself appear too knowledgeable of the inner workings of the turbines and generators. Besides, he had not made himself out as an expert in the mechanics of the powerstations. He provided just enough for Max to see him as a potential asset to his gang of conspirators. Fels stopped speaking and apologized for talking so long. He could tell that he had definitely garnered Max's attention.

Then Max abruptly ended the encounter. "Wil, I have a meeting shortly, but I would like to talk with you further. Could you meet me here tomorrow evening about this same time? Perhaps there are opportunities for you to consider."

Fels saw the seriousness Max was projecting. "Why, sure, I'd look forward to more conversation with you."

"It's settled, then. I will see you tomorrow. Now, my meeting is of a private nature. I'm sure you wouldn't mind leaving." Max had a broad, warm smile on his face. Fels rose from his chair and extended his hand. After a more friendly type of handshake from Max, Fels nodded at the man, then he turned and made his way to exit the tavern.

Later that night, hoping Blackmon's meeting had ended, Fels called him and asked if they could meet. Blackmon wanted some details, but Fels did not want to discuss it over the phone. So, Blackmon agreed to meet Fels at a small diner near Amherst, southeast of Tonawanda.

The two men arrived for a cup of coffee together. As it was getting late, the regular evening crowd had cleared out for the most part. They found a table near the back that was away from where most activity would normally be. The two men placed their orders after exchanging pleasantries.

"Tell me what's going on, Fels. Why couldn't you talk on the phone? What was so important that it couldn't wait until morning?" Blackmon was not really upset about being called out at the late hour, but he felt it was rather unusual.

"I'm just being cautious at this point." Fels looked around warily. "Remember the discussion we had after yesterday's surveillance of the tavern?"

"Yes, we agreed you would not go in alone."

"I didn't see it the same way."

"What do you mean?"

"Myron, he was there tonight!"

"You went there alone?! Fels, you should never have done that."

"The deadline's too near, Myron. I couldn't risk missing him, and it paid off."

"Fels, do you know how close I am to walking out right now?! We agreed—"

"No, we didn't! We both made our feelings known, but we did not agree!"

Blackmon turned away from Fels and threw up his hands in desperation. "Fels, you're splitting hairs. You're wrong, and you know it!" He turned back and glared at Fels.

"Myron, I won't apologize. You know there was little chance that I would be in any danger."

"I'm not happy, Fels."

"Well, maybe this will make you happy. As I started to say, he was there tonight—"

Blackmon looked up at the ceiling. "And I suppose you approached him?"

"He was alone, so, yes, I approached him. Don't worry. I was careful."

"Careful? Did he know you were a detective? Was he alone, or were there others there?"

"He was alone. There was no one else around at all. I handled it all just as we rehearsed. My cover story captivated him. I think I sold it well without arousing any suspicion."

"Fels, I still wish you hadn't proceeded like this without me. You can't take risks like this alone."

"Myron, I made myself look very appealing to him for what we both know his plans are. You know he needs the help with Sporco out of the picture."

"Alright, Fels, fill me in, and don't leave out any details. You know we can't take this to the Secret Service, and I must know everything that you discussed."

The two men spoke as they drank their coffee. Fels told Blackmon every bit of the conversation he had with Max. He finished by telling Blackmon that he would meet the man again tomorrow evening.

"So, what's your next move when you meet tomorrow?"

"Unless I have totally misread him, as I said, I believe Max bought my story. Assuming he needs to add another member to his cabal, I think I'm in a good position to be drawn in. Further assuming that he invites me in, I'll need to get his last name. Then you can check your BOI records to see if you have anything on him. From there, I hope to confirm the timeline and locations. That should substantiate the information I gathered from Sporco's tenement."

Blackmon agreed with Fels' approach. Fels agreed Blackmon would follow him to the meeting and surveil from a distance. Fels paid for the coffee, and the two departed ways until tomorrow.

CHAPTER 21

Wanting to appear ambitious, Fels arrived at the tavern fifteen minutes early for the meeting with Max the following day. He assumed correctly that Max would already be there waiting for him. Fels removed his hat and combed his fingers through his hair as he entered the tavern. He quickly scanned the room, noting one man at the bar and two men at a table across the room from Max, who was seated at the same table as before, near the fireplace at the back, and facing the entrance to the tavern. He recognized the two men at the table across the room. They were the same two men Fels had seen the first time at the table with Max, the men he had followed from Sporco's apartment.

Max lifted his eyes toward Fels but made no other indication to acknowledge him. Fels walked steadily across the room, his hat in his hands. Again, he wanted to appear eager, but not anxious. He could not allow Max to see any sense of nervousness, doubt, or fear. Fels only wanted to display confidence and readiness. As Fels neared the table, Max, with his right arm, motioned to the chair across from him. Fels slid the chair away from the table, calmly sat down, and placed his hat on the table as Max had apparently done.

"Wil, my good boy, I'm glad to see you are here ... and early." Max smiled at Fels and extended his hand. The two shook hands. The handshake was shorter this time, but it was still firm. Fels could feel Max's penetrating stare as he assessed him. Fels remained calm and confident, sitting forward in his chair.

"I'm eager to hear what you have to say. You made it sound as if there might be some sort of opportunity for someone like me—"

Max interrupted, "What do you mean, someone like you?"

"When we spoke, I shared my—uh, what's a good word—my discontent, meine unzufriedenheit, with my status as someone of German descent who is being looked down upon by these pompous Americans, most of whom came from somewhere else themselves." Fels showed a mild bit of anger. He didn't want to overplay his attitude, however. He also hoped adding the bit of German was not overselling.

"Yes, yes, I see." Max looked pensively and turned his head toward the ceiling as if searching for his next thought. His large belly rose as he moved. "Yes, I may have an opportunity for one such as yourself. You seem like an intelligent individual. Would you say that you are?"

"Yes, I guess so. As I told you, I'm quite good with mechanical things."

"You also seem to have a good awareness and a confident presence about you. You carry yourself well, and you have a good control over your emotions." Max looked at Fels with raised eyebrows.

"I am sorry for some of the anger that I showed at our last meeting. It's not typical of me to express myself like that, but I felt as if you were someone I could open up to." He spoke as if exposing his weakness to a trusted superior.

Max waved his hand back and forth. "No need for apologies. But let me ask you one very serious question." Max placed his hands together, and a scowl crossed his face. "Are you a police officer?" He watched Fels very carefully.

The question shocked Fels, but he did his best not to show it. At the same time, he knew he had to express some surprise. The real question in Fels' mind was whether Max knew something, or if he was just fishing. "What?! What do you mean, police officer?! I told you I worked at the power plant."

"I know what you told me. And now, I am asking this. Are you a police officer?" Max was calm and direct, implying that Fels was lying.

"Absolutely not! That's just crazy. Why would you even think such a thing? I don't understand."

"In my business, one cannot be too careful, Wil. Now, from what I have been able to glean, there is no one by the name of Wilhelm Roloff working at any of the power plants, at least not on the American side, which is where you told me you worked. So, if you are not a police officer, and if you do work at the power plant, can you explain? As I said, I can't be too careful." Max was now glaring at Fels.

"I mean, I don't know what I can do to convince you I'm telling you the truth. I am who I say I am." Fels retained the dumbfounded expression on his face while his mind turned over and over in search of his next statement.

At that moment, a man approached the table, looked at Fels, and said, "Wil Roloff, you stinking Hun. Wha'd they do, kick you out of the tool cage at the plant?" The man laughed heartily.

Fels replied to the man, "It's my day off."

"You and your Kaiser-loving buddies oughta stay locked in that cage as far as the rest of us are concerned." He scowled at Fels.

"Look, why don't you just leave?"

The man spat at Fels' feet. "Oh, I'm leaving alright. I don't care to drink at the same tavern as the likes of you." The man turned and walked out the door.

Fels was now really shocked. *Who was that? Maybe Blackmon sent him. But how would he ....*

"It appears my question has been answered, Herr Roloff." Max smiled in a way that Fels had never seen.

Fels was puzzled, but relieved. Max's concern had been completely silenced. Max's use of the German salutation seemed to indicate a sort of acceptance of Fels.

Fels shed the false air of disgust he had displayed toward the man. He faced Max with a look of renewed confidence. "I'm sorry about that, but you saw firsthand what I've been talking about." Fels paused. "I'm just sick of it. Something has to be done."

"Well, my boy, perhaps we can do something about that. However, I still need to understand why there is no record of your employment at the power plant." This time, Max's question felt less like an interrogation.

Fortunately, Fels had had a few moments to formulate an answer for Max. "I had forgotten about it over the years, but when I hired in at the plant, I used the name William Roberts. Like many Germans, I used an Americanized name to make myself more appealing as an employee. It was just about a year ago that the men at the plant found out my real name. They haven't let up on me since."

"I see." Max gave Fels a good look-over, searching for any sign of truth or falsehood in Fels' face or other body movements. He let out a heavy sigh, paused, and then said, "Let's get down to business, my boy."

Fels felt he had sold his story well enough that Max would not do any further checking on his employment records. If he was wrong, it would be disastrous for him.

"Wil, I am the owner of this establishment. I purchased it just over two years ago from the original owner. Of course, you know that story, and now you know who the current owner is. The tavern provides a good place to conduct my other business without arousing anyone's suspicions. We will meet from time to time out here in the open, but for the more discrete discussions, we will meet in my office in the back of the tavern."

Fels was quite surprised by Max's sudden turn, and he had obviously been made aware of Fels' earlier conversation with the bartender. Fels was glad that he had not pressed the bartender for more information.

With that, Max pushed himself away from the table. He nodded to the two men at the table across the room. They left their table and went through the door to the rear. "Follow me, Wil."

Fels was already standing as he had risen when Max stood. Fels followed as Max made his way slowly to the door. A sign on the door read, "PRIVATE." Passing through the door, the men entered a short hallway. Fels could see that at the end of the hallway was what appeared to be a stockroom for the tavern. Just to the right was an open door to a small office that appeared to be a manager's office for the business. To the left was a closed door with no window and no sign. Max opened the door and allowed Fels to enter before entering himself and closing the door behind him.

Upon entering the room, Fels saw the two men sitting at a large rectangular table, a table as might be located in a business office conference room. The furniture in the room was much finer than anything in the barroom area. A small bar to one side contained bottles of the finest of liquors. A large ornate desk had no clutter, holding a telephone, a pad of paper, and a pen in a pen holder. There was art on the walls that appeared to be of fine quality to Fels' untrained eye. Some sort of fine tapestry completely covered the wall at the rear of the room. It was all quite ornate, just bordering on being over-the-top.

"Please, sit, Wil."

Wil sat in the chair that Max had indicated for him. It was opposite of the two men on the other side of the table. Max settled into a large padded chair at the head of the table. "Before we can begin, Wil, please tell us about the powerstation where you work." He had motioned to the other two men as he made the request.

Fels was ready with his background story. "Sure. Well, I started out at Schoellkopf's Plant No. 2." He used some of his actual background in discussing growing up on the farm and his interest in how things worked. He keyed in on his father's love for the German homeland. He explained how his father had insisted that the family speak German at home. He expanded the story to include the singing of old German songs as a family tradition. It was a real opportunity to express a deep tie to the German way of life.

Fels then noted the falling out he had with his father and his lack of desire to continue in the farming way of life. His interests led him to a casual repair business of his own, which grew to the point that he left the farm entirely. The opportunity for better wages while using his mechanical skills eventually led him to the job with the Niagara Power Company at Plant No. 2.

Max remained keenly focused on every word that Fels spoke. He was looking for anything that might indicate a lie in Fels' story. Because Fels had used so much of his actual background, Max saw nothing in Fels' face or demeanor to show he might be lying. Max interrupted Fels' story a few times, asking for additional details in an attempt to trip him up, but Fels easily handled every question.

Fels finished his story with some final comments about the views of Germans now being expressed by so many so-called Americans, most of them from immigrant families themselves. Fels closed with a final statement. "Max, I am just sick of it. I mean, you saw how I was treated." He paused as if searching the depths of his brain for the right words. "You know, Max, as bad as it is for me, and all Germans in America, I can't help but think of the German people in the homeland who are facing the wrath of the imperialist nation of Great Britain. I would do anything to help these people." Fels stopped as if he was spent from the despair he had described.

Max smiled broadly across the table at Fels. "Wil, my boy, welcome to our group. I believe you are ready to understand our objective. Wil, if you truly believe everything you have told me—"

"Of course I do!" Fels hoped he hadn't sounded too eager.

"Good, my boy. Then it is time to engage you with our team. Wil, we are going to do something to address the very issues you have expressed such great concern about. I mean, we are taking real action. We are done with talking."

Fels leaned forward with great interest.

"Wil, across the table are Peter Niemand and Otto Bergman. These two men have been in my employ for quite some time. They are loyal men willing to take whatever steps are necessary to assist those good German folks that you referenced. They are good soldiers." The men simply nodded their heads toward Fels, and he returned the same. "Wil, are you prepared to be a good soldier for those good German people in the homeland?" As Max spoke, his eyes were nearly glowing with pride.

Fels leaned forward. "I am ready, Max!"

Max continued, "We have a plan of action. Real action. Meaningful action! And, Wil, this is not merely a local action. No, I am under the direct command of the highest levels of German military intelligence.

"Wil, we recently lost one of our men in a tragic accident. He had a very key role in our operation. Fortunately, he had completed the most important part of his assignment. However, we need a good soldier to fill his role in part two of the plan. Now, for me to continue, I must have your sworn allegiance to this project and to the German military establishment. You must never speak of this with anyone outside this room." Now Max paused for effect. He looked deeply into Fels' eyes. "Defiling your oath and allegiance to this project will require the ultimate payment. Do you understand, my boy?"

"Yes, I think I get it. I'm all in, Max."

"Very good. Very good. I will continue."

Max started at the top. Max shared with Fels how everything tiered up to Section 3-B, the highest German military intelligence organization. The German Ambassador to the United States, Count Johann von Bernstorff, located in Washington D.C., was actually a trained espionage agent. He was, in fact, Germany's espionage and sabotage chief for the entire Western Hemisphere. To support his effort, he was assisted by Captain Franz von Papen, currently military attaché in Mexico who transferred to the United States, Captain Karl Boy-Ed, naval attaché, and Dr. Heinrich Albert, the commercial attaché who was handling the finances for the sabotage operations. With this small group of men, Bernstorff was carrying out the German strategy against the United States.

Fels used every bit of control he could muster to keep from showing the shock he had just experienced. Max had confirmed everything that Agent Wilson had shared, but with much more detail. This thing was much bigger than what he had expected. It did indeed tier up to the highest level of German military intelligence. He suppressed every urge to jump up from the table and take Max as a prisoner. It was vital that Fels contact Blackmon as soon as he could. He kept the impact of this pushed down inside himself, however. He needed more information, and he could show no hint of the emotions he was feeling.

The project Max was discussing was under the command of Captain von Papen. Von Papen was currently located in New York City, overseeing several projects to undermine the ability of the United States to provide support to Great Britain against the German people. There was continued emphasis on the provision of aid to the German citizenry. There was no real mention of backing the German military intentions. The object of Germany, at this time, was to keep the United States neutral and, at the same time, to impede the flow of war materials and food supplies from North America to the allied powers.

Von Papen had a network of cohorts engaged in a variety of subversive activities in the United States. Besides the plans to blow up the powerstations along the Niagara River, there were plans to destroy the locks along the Welland Canal, plans to place explosives on ships leaving American ports, and plans to foment labor unrest that would impede the export of munitions and other supplies to Great Britain. This was a far-reaching operation.

Max arrived at his particular assignment in the German espionage plans directly from von Papen. The powerstations were to be targeted at the same time as the Welland Canal, creating a double blow to the United States' capabilities to support Great Britain. The destruction of the canal would directly affect shipments out of the United States. There would be a two-fold impact from the destruction of the powerstations. It would create a power outage disrupting manufacturing processes of all sorts. Cutting off both the supply and the supply route would deal an enormous blow to American support for Great Britain. Secondly, it would be a part of the overall objective to create a panic among the American people, a panic that should bring into question the very idea of supporting Great Britain's war effort.

Max finished up by letting everyone know that even he was not aware of all the projects being undertaken. It was best that each team was unaware of the details of any other team. In this way, if any part of the overall plan was stopped, no one would be able to provide any knowledge of the other plans if interrogated. Yes, the German minds were far superior to the American minds.

Max made no mention of the failure of the Welland Canal plot or the powerstations on the Canadian side of the Niagara. Perhaps he was not aware, but Fels thought it more likely that he did not want to admit to a German failure of a part of the plot. He felt Max did not want to do anything that might undermine his own operation or display a weakness in the German plans. For Max, everything was a go for this operation.

CHAPTER 22

"Myron, I'm in!"

"Fill me in—and don't leave out any details."

Both men were eager to discuss the details of Fels' meeting with Max.

"First. let me thank you for sending in your man to pose as my co-worker. That—"

"What man? I didn't send anyone in."

"But the tall dark-haired man who came in about a half-hour after I arrived. He came over to the table where Max and I were talking. Myron, Max was asking if I was a police officer. I was trying to explain when this man came over who said he was a co-worker at the power plant." Fels stopped and saw the empty look on Blackmon's face. "You didn't send him in, did you?"

"No. And I don't remember seeing anyone come in after you."

They both stared blankly at one another. Then Myron broke the silence. "Fels, someone knows what's going on."

"But that can't be. I've told no one but you, and I assumed you told no one. But, did you have to read someone in at the BOI?"

"No. Like you, I've spoken of this to no one."

Both men felt the blood draining from their blank faces. Fels turned his head ever so slightly from side to side. His face softened and an imperceptible smile briefly expressed itself. "I think I know who it was. We're okay." Fels had fully regained his confidence.

"Fels, who else have you brought in? You know very well you should have told me," scolded Blackmon.

Fels recognized Blackmon was upset. "I'm sorry, Myron. You're gonna have to trust me on this one."

"Trust you?! I've shown nothing but trust in you, Fels. I've stuck my neck out here. I haven't even told my boss in New York City. Fels, if this goes sideways, my job is on the line. Do you understand?! Now tell me who this is." Blackmon was now looking sternly into Fels' eyes.

Fels knew Blackmon was losing his patience. "Look, Myron, it's someone who's watching out for me. I didn't know he'd show up there." Fels knew he was getting nowhere with his weak explanation. "Believe me. He won't tell anyone what's going on, and he won't do anything to expose us. I know I'm not giving you much, but again, I'm asking you to trust me on this."

"Fels, I do trust you. What I don't trust is the unknown, and this man is an unknown to me. Fels, I cannot —I will not—operate in the dark. Now, tell me who he is!"

"I'm sorry you're angry about this—"

"Darn right, I'm angry. If all you're saying is true—and I have assumed that to be the case up to now—then we are in a very risky position. And we have no back-up." Blackmon turned his face away from Fels.

"Okay, okay. His name is David. He's kinda helped me out in certain situations in the past. I didn't recognize him today. I was very nervous, and he was well-disguised."

"How did he know you'd be here today?"

"I didn't tell him. He knows I've been working on something big. I guess he just followed me. The disguise was so I wouldn't recognize him. I'm really sorry about this, Myron, but everything is okay. You know, he saved my butt in there."

"I don't like this, Fels. No more surprises. Talk to your man, and tell him to stay out of this!"

"I'll talk to him, but he might be able to help us out. I mean, he's already inserted himself. Maybe we can use him."

Myron turned his head from side to side. "Talk to him. Is he capable?"

"Well, you saw how his disguise fooled me. Yes, he's capable."

"What about his background? Does he have any law enforcement experience?"

"Only what he's picked up from me, but I've known him for a very long time."

"Fels, one wrong move, one mistake, and he's gone— and so am I. There's only so far I'm willing to stick my neck out. Understood?"

"Yeah, we're good."

In his controlled and organized manner, Blackmon felt this discussion was over, and he was ready to move forward. "Now, tell me more about your meeting."

Fels relayed the details of the meeting. He had gotten the man's full name, Maximilian Strasse. "He tossed out some other names. It seems he has ties that go back to the German Ambassador to the United States, Johann von Bernstorff."

"From what I know, that's not surprising. The German Ambassador has been under scrutiny by a dedicated group of BOI agents, as well as the Secret Service. He's currently back in Germany."

"I was able to get one more name, Franz von Papen. Apparently, he was running Max's plan from Mexico, but he's now in New York City."

"Now we have something. Von Papen's name was associated with the Welland Canal plot based on what the Secret Service shared with us. This means Max and his associates are likely separate from the group who plotted the Welland Canal plan. If that's the case, then the Secret Service really does think they have everything under control. They aren't aware that these are two very close plots organized completely separate from each other. So, if one group is exposed, it does not link to the other group. At least they can still execute half of their plan. What else have you got?"

"The rest is not so good, I think. I'm meeting the rest of the group tomorrow, but the best I can tell is the date of November 24 is firm."

"Fels, that's only about two weeks away. I was hoping we might get an extension with the loss of Sporco."

"I know, and if we take this to the Secret Service with no concrete evidence, they'll toss us out on our butts. I just don't see how we can get any concrete evidence to take to them. Max had no papers with him as he spoke. All we have is my conversation with Max."

"You're right. They'll never listen to us. Fels,—"

Fels interrupted, "It's up to you and me to stop this."

They looked at one another. Both men knew they were in this alone. Both knew that the consequences of not succeeding would be devastating. Failure was simply not an option. They both had a renewed sense of duty ... to their friends and neighbors, to Blackmon's family, to the people of Niagara and the surrounding area, to the United States of America. Fresh energy and clear purpose bolstered their resolve and prepared them to move forward with bold courage.

The following day, Blackmon began his research into the name Maximilian Strasse. By the end of the day, he had put together a surprising background on the man. He had several aliases he had used over the past ten years. Most recently, he had used the name Massi, a shortened version of Massimiliano, an Italian name, and the surname of Strada. Before that, he had used several Italian aliases. The BOI had had Strada under investigation in relation to the Italian control of the docks in Buffalo. By the time Blackmon had been assigned to his role in the BOI in Buffalo, Strada had disappeared. He was not someone Blackmon had ever investigated in his activities with the Mafia's accounting records.

Strada, according to the records Blackmon had uncovered, worked directly with the mob bosses to establish an import business. He was thought to have established schemes to undervalue shipments and reclassify the goods being imported. Strada was able to ensure a nice profit for the mob while bringing his products in at a very low price, thus enabling him to make large margins on sales of the goods.

The BOI had investigated the use of false invoices and other schemes to defraud. Apparently, Strada and the Mafia had done a good job of covering everything with a separate set of books that were never located. They eventually dropped the investigation. The name Massi Strada failed to show up on any subsequent investigations. It appeared as though the man had disappeared. This was nearly four years ago, about the time Blackmon had been assigned to the Buffalo BOI office.

Blackmon figured that at the time Max began his import business with the Mafia, it was best to do so as an Italian, hence the use of the Italian alias. Things were starting to heat up for the Mafia about four years ago as

Blackmon began his work and as Fels was becoming disturbed by the corruption in the Buffalo Police Department. He now presumed that Max had reestablished his business using his apparent real name, the German Maximilian Strasse. From what Fels had learned, it appeared as though Shorty's Tavern was a front from which to run his business enterprises.

There was nothing to indicate that Max was heavily concerned about the plight of the Germans back in Germany. There was nothing that would indicate that he was concerned about Great Britain getting the support of the United States. No, it was more likely that his interests were in making money and growing his personal power base. His only genuine interest was going to be in himself alone. He would use others to promote himself, regardless of the consequences for the others.

Max's business ties to the Mafia left Blackmon concerned. Blackmon felt there was at least some possibility that Max could uncover the link between Fels and the work he had done breaking up a Mafia robbery ring while at the Buffalo PD. So far, there was no reason to expect that Max had made any connection, but it left Blackmon with a general uneasiness.

Blackmon shared his concern with Fels. "If Max is aware of anything about your work in breaking up that gang, it could mean grave danger for you. If he takes you by surprise at the tavern, I might not even be aware that he had done so. Fels, maybe we should take what we have to Agent Wilson—"

"No! You know he won't hear us out, but he will toss us out. You've made me aware of the concern. It's a reasonable risk to take at this point. There isn't time to make an alternate play."

"Okay. I know you're right, but just know I will be watching your back closely. I would feel terrible if anything were to happen to you."

"Well, if it should, at least someone might listen to you!" Fels tried to lighten the mood by laughing at his own comment. Blackmon just shook his head.

CHAPTER 23

Max spoke, "As you are aware, we lost a critical member of our team with Mr. Sporco's untimely death. In addition to his bomb-making expertise, he was to lead our attack on the Schoellkopf powerstations below the falls." Max interrupted himself to take a deep, wheezy breath. Around the table, paying attention to Max's every word, were Fels, Otto Bergman, Peter Niemand, Robert Werner, and a new face that Fels met for the first time, John Meno. "While we have added Wil to our ranks, I feel it is too risky to proceed with that portion of the plan." Another raspy breath. "However, gentlemen, we will not let our homeland down. Our task is critical to delaying America's support to Britain in the war." He looked each of the men directly in the eyes with all the seriousness he could muster. "We must remain committed!"

As he finished, Max slapped an open palm down on the table. The men all held back any shock they may have felt from Max's fiery action. They looked about at one another and began nodding their heads in complete agreement. Max then poured a glass of Ratzeputz German schnaps for each man at the table. He lifted his glass and proposed a toast. "For the homeland!" They each quickly downed the glass of the sharp ginger spirit in front of them.

Max slammed his glass down on the table. "Good! Let's get down to work. First, Mr. Werner has assured me that all the bombs are ready and in his possession. Mr. Sporco completed them before his untimely death. Mr. Werner will be in charge of delivering the explosives with the assistance of Mr. Bergmann." His eyes shifted between Robert Werner and Otto Bergmann. Both men nodded their heads in agreement. Max smiled.

Max removed a roll of papers from his desk and spread a map out onto the table. He slowly explained to the men their targets. He showed two key areas where explosives would be placed at the hydraulic canal. One was near the entrance of the canal just west of the two Niagara Falls Power Company powerstations, and the other was at a dogleg about a quarter of the way down the canal. Both would provide for maximum destruction and complicate restoration. This action would shut down all water flow to the Schoellkopf turbines.

Jacob Schoellkopf purchased the 4400-foot hydraulic canal in 1877. After several improvements, Schoellkopf had water flowing over the edge of the gorge below the falls to turbines, a sight that was as spectacular as the falls themselves. Schoellkopf realized the future of harnessing the power of Niagara was in the commercial production of electricity. He adapted this available electrical technology to his powerhouse turbines, and one of the first hydro-electric generating stations in the world was born.

Max then opened a map of the Niagara Falls Power Company powerstations. There would be no change to blowing up the two stations. What would change was the addition of explosive charges to destroy the head of the hydraulic tunnel. With both the canal and the tunnel out of commission, the plan would be every bit as devastating as taking out the Schoellkopf stations at the end of the canal. In fact, Max felt this plan was far better than the original. He smiled to himself with pride. He looked about the room, seeking acknowledgment on the faces of the men that he alone had indeed improvised an improved plan. To the man, they expressed their satisfaction with head nods.

Max's stubby fingers pointed to the map on the table. "Wil, since you are familiar with the powerstations, I am counting on you to take care of the tunnel. Perhaps you know its weakest point where we can be most effective?" He lifted his eyes to Fels.

"Max, as I've said, I just handle some basic maintenance—"

"Are you telling me you are of no use to this plan?!" Once again, Max slammed his hand on the table.

"Oh, by no means! What I was going to say was that while I handle basic maintenance, I hear things. Let me give it a little thought—"

"We don't have a lot of time, Wil!"

"I understand. I mean, just a day to think it through."

"You have until tomorrow afternoon. You will bring me the best alternative tomorrow!" Perspiration had begun to bead on Max's frowning brow.

"That won't be a problem." Fels spoke with a strong reassurance.

They reviewed the locations of where to place the explosives at the two powerstations themselves. Fels saw the full plan for the first time. Two men who had been assigned to the Schoellkopf stations were reassigned to the hydraulic canal. The assignments for the two other men remained unchanged to plant the explosives at the two powerstations. And, the new addition to the plan was to have Fels place explosives at the head of the hydraulic tunnel one-hundred-sixty feet below ground.

With plans finalized and assignments confirmed, Max sent the men back into the tavern at staggered intervals. They were to order a beer and leave separately when they were finished.

Max stopped Wil as he was about to leave the room and leaned in toward his ear. "Wil, you convinced me of your resolve to support Germany in this effort. Should you have second thoughts, it might not go well for you." Max backed off and stared deeply and coldly at Fels as he wiped his brow.

"No, Max, I understand. I did not intend to show any hesitation." Fels perked up. "I want to be sure this is done right and inflicts maximum damage. I'm all in. You can count on me." Fels held his head high in a stance of pride.

"Tomorrow afternoon, Wil, tomorrow afternoon." His penetrating stare continued.

Fels met Blackmon an hour later at a small restaurant in Tonawanda. "Myron, we need some basic information on the tunnel at the Niagara Falls Power Company. I have to prepare something reasonable for Max and these other men."

"I have someone I can speak with."

"It's got to be done by tomorrow morning. I have to have a plan for Max by tomorrow afternoon." Fels was concerned but not panicked.

"I'll handle it. Let's meet here for lunch. That should give you enough time to get back to Max."

At that, Fels provided Blackmon with all the details from the meeting. The circumstances certainly provided a challenge for the two men.

"Look, Max has two men at two different locations at the canal. Then there is a man at each of the powerstations. Now, I'll be there as well, but Myron, you and I are just not enough."

"I have to agree. We'll never get the attention of the Secret Service without actual evidence, however. Is there anyone at all from your department that you think you could bring in?"

"I'm not in good stead with anyone right now ... except for Chief Bruckhart ... maybe. But I'm afraid trying to bring the chief in could be problematic." Fels stopped, and Blackmon stared at him, expressing that he could not agree with Fels' assessment of Chief Bruckhart. "Really, Myron? That's a big ask."

"I know, but what other choice do we have? I have no men whatsoever available. It's only me for another four-to-six weeks."

"This could backfire on us. Chief Bruckhart could slap cuffs on me and lock me up. Then he'd call the director of the BOI!" Fels couldn't help but laugh at the thought. Blackmon even cracked a smile.

Fels called Chief Bruckhart first thing the next morning. The chief was more than happy to meet with Fels. Fels had only mentioned that there was something of importance he needed to discuss. The chief had asked Fels if he needed Captain Flynn to meet with them as well. Fels had told him that, no, this was something he needed to discuss alone. Fels went so far as to ask if they could meet outside of the precinct for breakfast. The chief had enough respect for Fels that he agreed without reservation.

Following the requisite small talk, Fels got down to business. "Chief, I have a big ask of you."

"Fels, whatever you need. I know I had to come down a bit strong because of the, uh, dispute with Agent Wilson, but we're good."

"That's good to know. Now, please hold your comments until I have given you all the information."

The chief cocked his head sideways. "Okay."

"I know you don't want to hear this, but BOI Agent Blackmon and I have continued investigating the plot to blow up the American powerstations."

"Fels!"

"Please, sir, hear me out. Look, both of us could not shake this thing. From everything we saw following the meeting and the news, it does not appear that the Secret Service has uncovered the American side of the plot."

Chief Bruckhart leaned back in his chair and pondered the ceiling.

Fels continued. "Chief, this thing is real. We have worked our way into the actual group planning to destroy two powerstations, the canal, and the hydraulic tunnel."

The chief leaned forward. "What are you telling me?"

"Chief, we are in with the group—I am in the group. We know the entire plan and timeline! I've inserted myself into their organization. And this is going to happen November 24 unless we can stop it."

"Fels, we've got to take this to Agent Wilson!"

"Chief, we have nothing to take to him. All we have is my word backed by Agent Blackmon. Does that sound like anything new and different? We'd be tossed out on our butts. You'd be asked to fire me, and I'm sure the BOI would fire Myron."

"Hmm, I don't disagree. What do you suggest?"

"The plan is laid out. We can stop it, but we need more than just myself and Myron. I think Myron and I can handle the powerstations and the tunnel. In fact, I'm the one who is to place the explosives in the tunnel; that one is easily taken care of. We need men at the canal. They are planting explosives at two locations. If you can have men waiting there for them, we can stop this thing."

The chief listened closely as Fels provided all the details. The chief agreed to provide enough men at the canal locations. They would arrive early and lay in wait for Max's men. Chief Bruckhart agreed that this needed to be done with the fewest number of patrolmen involved, and they would be required to keep the arrangements under wraps. If any word at all got out, it could be disastrous.

"Chief, thank-you! As I said, I know this is a big ask. But, I think you'll agree it is of great importance to the country. I'd like to bring in Agent Wilson, but we both know what would happen if we approached him with this. Look, I have to go. Myron is getting some information for me, and then I have a meeting with Max. I'll give you the rest of the details later."

Chief Bruckhart slid back his chair and stood, walked over to Fels, and shook his hand. "I know how difficult this must have been for you. Thanks for following that Krieger instinct you have and not letting this rest. We'll owe a great debt of gratitude to you when this thing has been stopped and the men have been brought to justice." The handshake was followed by an encouraging slap on the back as the men left the restaurant.

CHAPTER 24

It was November 23, and in one hour it would be the start of the day of the bombing—the day before the Day of Thanksgiving. Fels arrived at Shorty's tavern at 11:00 p.m. Max had moved the meeting up to an earlier time. Fels assumed he wanted to go over the details of the plan with everyone one more time. The plan was to have the men enter the powerstations and canal at 2:00 a.m. in the morning and place the bombs with timers to explode at 7:00 a.m. That would give the men plenty of time to place the bombs and leave the area. This was to be a devastating event, killing the powerstation crew when they arrived in the morning, as well as taking out the turbines, the tunnel, and the canal.

Fels entered the tavern at exactly 11:00 p.m. and made his way to the back room. When he entered, Max was in his usual chair at the head of the table, and two other men were seated, one on each side of the table. Fels had never seen these men at anytime in the tavern, and certainly not in any of their meetings. They were both large men who looked like they could have been dock workers. For all his exercise at Turner's, Fels' physique didn't begin to compare to the powerful bodies of these two men. Fels quickly assessed them as muscle for Max, but he didn't understand why they were here tonight.

"Good evening, Wil. Please take a seat." Max gestured to the far side of the table with his outstretched arm. A broad smile had appeared and remained on his face as he focused on Wil.

Fels made his way around the table and sat in the only other chair next to one of the Tarzan-like men. While both of these men were quiet, they appeared a bit nervous to Fels.

"I hope I'm not too early. I thought I was right on time." Fels addressed Max apologetically, as if he had entered a meeting that he was not supposed to be in.

"Oh no, my boy, your timing couldn't be better. The others should be here shortly. This is an important night for all of us, and for the Motherland." The smile still on his face, Max looked at each man in turn.

The door opened, and another man entered. Fels did not recognize him from any of the meetings he had attended. He, like the others, had the appearance of a dock worker. Fels did not like this surprise and was feeling uncomfortable. He tried not to show any concern, but he didn't like seeing a new face. He nodded his head at the man, who stared momentarily at Fels and then approached Max. He leaned over and whispered into Max's ear. Max smiled again.

This other man moved around the table, pulled a chair over, and sat down next to Fels. Fels kept his focus on Max and did not look at any of the others. He felt something was off, but he couldn't quite put his finger on it.

"Well, what do you say we begin?" Max said matter-of-factly.

Fels was puzzled. *How can we begin without the others?*

Fels was suddenly grabbed by the two men, the one on his right and the other on his left.

"What's going on?!" Fels was caught by surprise, and the two men easily subdued him.

"Indeed, my boy, just what is going on?" There was no longer a smile on Max's face. He was enraged. As he spoke, spittle gathered at the corners of his mouth. "Tell me, Wil, or should I say Detective Krieger, what ... is ... going ... on?!" He slammed his fist on the table.

Fels' heart skipped a beat. He had to think quickly. "I don't know what you mean! Who is this detective you seem to think I am?"

Max rose from his chair more quickly than Fels had ever seen him move. "No more lies!!" He moved across the table from Fels as he spoke. He leaned on the table to get his reddened face as close to Fels as he could. "Tell me why I shouldn't kill you right now!"

It was then that Fels noticed the gun in Max's hand. Max straightened up, raised the gun, and pointed it squarely at Fels' head. Fels tried to break his arms free, but the two men were strong and had him well-confined to the chair.

"Look, Max—"

"I said no more lies! Do you understand?! I know you are Detective Felsen Krieger of the Tonawanda Police Department, formerly a member of the Buffalo Police Department, the same Felsen Krieger who rounded up a Mafia-organized robbery ring." Max had to stop and breathe deeply. "Do you take me for a fool?!"

It was the one nagging uneasiness that Blackmon had mentioned as a concern to Fels. He had felt there was at least some possibility that Max could uncover the link between Fels and the work he had done breaking up a Mafia robbery ring while at the Buffalo PD. Now, it seemed like that was exactly what Max had figured out. Fels' heart sank.

"Tie him up!" Max barked at the other three men.

The two continued to hold him while the third man lifted a rope that he had on his lap under the table. Fels again tried to struggle, but to no avail, as they tied his hands behind his back and his feet together to the chair. The powerful thugs then moved him away from the table to the front of Max's desk.

"Now, let's get some questions answered, shall we, Detective Krieger?" As he said this, he motioned to the three men to exit the room. Max was obviously quite comfortable that he had the upper hand with Fels well-constrained. He walked around the chair and examined Fels' ropes. He returned to the front of his desk and faced Fels. Fels had tried to keep his hands expanded and away from the chair as much as he could when they tied him, but he now realized that he was tightly bound.

"So, tell me, Detective Krieger, who have you told about our project?" His lips were dry while spittle continued collecting at the corners of his mouth. His face was still red, and his brow was covered with perspiration.

"You seem to have it all figured out. If so, then you know that I'm acting alone on this." Fels tried to remain calm and appear to be straightforward with Max.

Max slapped Fels across the face. "I said no more lies!! Do you not understand?! You are a detective, formerly with the Buffalo Police Department, and now with the Tonawanda Police Department. You are currently on leave as you recover from injuries and from the loss of your family in an explosion at your home. You, yes, you, uncovered Paul Sporco as the individual responsible for that explosion! You pursued him and killed him at the falls. Is this starting to sound familiar now?!" He slapped Fels again and wiped his mouth with his coat sleeve.

"As I said, it appears you have it all figured out." This time, Max hit him across the face with his gun.

"Well, you see, if you have told anyone ... well, the plans have changed." Max seemed to settle down. "Detective, the bombs have all been put in place already. While you thought you arrived just on time tonight, you actually arrived far too late. How unfortunate for you. Oh, and the timers are set for 2:00 a.m. So, if anyone is arriving at that time thinking they will stop my men, how unfortunate for them!" Max laughed viciously. Sweat was dripping from the tip of his nose.

Max slipped his gun into his coat pocket and walked over to the bar. He removed a bottle from the shelf and poured himself a drink. He threw the liquid down his throat, poured another drink, and did the same.

"Did you really think that no one would recognize you?! The new man you met, Mr. Meno, well, he told me he thought he recalled your face from somewhere, but he couldn't quite put his finger on it. He was loyal enough to me to express his concern. Two days ago, he remembered. You see, Mr. Meno was with the gang of thieves you arrested when you were with the Buffalo PD. Well, how fortunate for me to have Mr. Meno identify you. And, how unfortunate for you, detective!" A vengeful smile crossed Max's face.

Max took the bottle in his hand and walked back to Fels. "You would probably like one of these to settle your nerves, yes, detective? Let's see what I can do for you, shall we?" He lifted the bottle above his head and smashed it to the floor at Fels' feet. "Oh, my! I am so sorry, my boy. The bottle seems to have slipped from my hand. Let me get another." He laughed like a man laughing at one of his own jokes.

Max grabbed two more bottles from the bar. "Ah, yes. Now, this is some very good vodka. Look at that." He held one of the bottles in front of Fels' face. Max was breathing heavily, almost wheezing. "One-hundred and sixty proof!" He smashed the two bottles at Fels' feet as he had with the first bottle. His ominous laugh was pure evil. "One-hundred and sixty proof! Highly flammable, you know!" His laughter caused him to cough. He reached out and leaned on his desk as he brought himself under control. "Oh, yes, I am enjoying this!"

Fels was now fully aware of Max's plan for him. He struggled in the chair, but it only confirmed that he was tightly bound. It was taking all of his fortitude not to panic.

"Struggling will not do you any good, my boy. My men know how to tie knots. They're German sailors, you see. Yes, good knots, good knots." Max chuckled to himself.

"Did you think you were up against a few disgruntled Germans?! Ha! This is bigger ... much, much bigger." Max held himself up as straight as he could, attempting to puff out his chest. "Remember, I work directly for the German Military Attaché, Franz von Papen! And, he in turn, reports to none other than the German Ambassador to the United States, Count Johann von Bernstorff! These assignments have been handed down from German Military Intelligence. You see, my boy, I am a very important part of this German show of strength! It was I who was recruited to carry out this key plan! Me! My import business has allowed other plans to develop as I provided the necessary materials. I will be well rewarded when this is complete! I have done something others have failed at!"

As Max was self-congratulating himself, his ego was pushing him to provide some very important information to Fels. That was all well and good, but, *How do I get out of these ropes and overpower Max? I've got to get to Blackmon.*

Max gathered his breath and mopped his brow with his handkerchief. "You were such a fool, my boy, to think that you could stop this finely crafted German plan." Another deep breath and another swipe across the brow. "And it is my understanding there are other sabotage plots underway across the country. America will be laid helpless to support Great Britain in the war against Germany!

"I personally recruited the men to partake in this operation. I planned this to the last detail!" He paused, and Fels could see that he was preparing to raise his voice. "Then you came along and killed my bomb maker!" Max raised his hand and slapped Fels once again. "You cost me time and money! But you will not cost me this operation!" One more slap to the side of Fels' head nearly knocked him over in the chair.

"There is still a chance for you to live, my boy. Tell me who else knows of this. Tell me, and you can escape with your life. Otherwise, you will be an intruder who died in his own attempt at arson. What will it be?" Max looked exhausted as he sat against the desk, breathing heavily.

"I told you, there is no one else. But, I do know how the Welland Canal operation was stopped. Maybe you didn't know that, Max? I know the man who stopped that as well as other plots. You are bound to fail!"

Max showed surprise. His face reddened, and he leaped to his feet. "You are lying! More lies! You've made your choice. You will die here tonight! I will not fail!!"

By now, Max had sweat through his jacket, and sweat was rolling off his face. Max walked behind his desk and picked up two large bottles. "My best bourbon, just for you, my boy." Once again, Max broke into laughter. He removed the cap from one of the bottles and passed it under Fels' nose.

Fels recoiled at the smell. *Gasoline!* Max laughed hysterically.

"Perhaps ... a little ... too ... fine ... for you?!" Max worked the words in with his uncontrollable laughter. He added some of the gasoline to the already-flammable mix at Fels' feet.

Then Max poured some gasoline on the ropes binding Fels' feet and hands. "The ropes will burn away, leaving no trace of your having been tied to the chair. Beautiful, don't you agree?"

Fels was bruised and frightened. *Perhaps it's right that I should die in a fire, as I should have the night my family was killed.* He actually felt some momentary solace in this thought.

He remained calm on the outside, as he didn't want to provide Max with any sense of satisfaction. *If David was going to help me out, he certainly would have been here by now. I don't understand his role and his work. I guess that truly is much bigger than I am.*

Max walked back behind his desk, grabbed his hat, placed it carefully on his sweaty head, and picked up the bottles of gasoline. He stopped in front of Fels. He said nothing. He spat at Fels' feet, then laughed one more time before exiting the room. He turned left in the hallway. Fels saw him splashing some of the gasoline before he made his way to the rear exit of the tavern. Fels heard Max smash the bottles of gasoline at the back door. Shortly thereafter, he heard a loud whoosh as the gasoline ignited.

CHAPTER 25

Chief Bruckhart had assembled two teams of men at the two canal locations that Fels had indicated would be targeted. To avoid any chance of being seen, Bruckhart and his men had been in place since just after sunset. They settled into their surroundings, carefully camouflaged, and patiently waited. They were to arrest the men when they approached quietly so as not to arouse any others in the plot who may be nearby as they approached the powerstations.

The bombers came into view about 9:00 p.m. They approached their targets casually, doing their best to appear to be simple men who might be going to or coming from work. They both carried lunch boxes and satchels, the obvious containers of the explosives.

They made the arrests quietly as the men were quickly controlled and their bags and pails were carefully whisked away by assigned patrolmen. Chief Bruckhart was a bit surprised by how early the men had appeared. From what Fels had told him, they would likely approach the canal around 2:00 a.m. He was glad that they had been ready at the earlier time. It all went down smoothly, and Chief Bruckhart assumed the same must be happening at the powerstations.

With everything handled even better than expected, the chief returned with his men to the station to begin processing the saboteurs. He was looking forward to contacting Agent Wilson after they had wrapped everything up.

Agent Blackmon arrived at the entrance of Powerstation No. 2 right at midnight. There was no need to arrive early and hide himself. There were plenty of shadowy areas to provide cover near the entrance. The canal was far enough away that Blackmon could not see any activity taking place there, and he would not be able to leave and provide assistance, in any case. He and Fels were the only ones to cover the powerstations.

He and Fels had agreed to meet at midnight. Fels was now thirty minutes late. It was unlike him, and Blackmon was getting nervous. Just then, he saw a figure approaching in the dark. He assumed it was Fels, but Blackmon kept himself concealed just in case it was not Fels. As the figure got close, Blackmon could see that it was indeed not Fels.

Blackmon slowly removed a .38 caliber Colt Police Positive pistol from his Lewis shoulder holster and stepped out from the shadows. He raised the 4-inch-barreled weapon with two hands and told the man to stop and identify himself.

"Please, Agent Blackmon, I have come here on behalf of Detective Krieger." The man was calm, almost polite.

"Who are you?"

"My name is David Smith. I am a friend of Detective Krieger, and he has asked me to help him out to stop the bombing tonight."

"And just where is Detective Krieger, Mr. Smith?" Blackmon kept his weapon steadily fixed on the man.

"He has been detained by Max. He wanted me to get to you in the event of something like this happening." The man continued calmly, "There is something you need to know—"

"What I want to know is why I should believe you." Blackmon was strong and insistent.

"I can assure you that I am who I say I am. I am the one who helped Fels out at the tavern that day when he met with Max. You will believe me when I tell you what is going on."

"Okay, convince me." Blackmon continued to keep his weapon pointed at David.

"Detective Krieger truly has been detained, and more importantly, the bombs have already been placed at the powerstations. Max figured out what was going on, and he had the bombs placed early. They are also set to go off earlier than planned. Agent Blackmon, we have less than an hour to locate and disarm the bombs."

Blackmon had a strong sense that the man was being completely honest. He felt as if he was talking with an old partner. Despite not being able to explain it, he had absolutely no reason to doubt the man. He re-holstered his pistol.

"Tell me what I need to know ... and is Fels on his way?"

"He was detained by Max, and he will not be here in time to help us. It's up to you and me, Agent Blackmon."

"Well, we have a lot of ground to cover—"

"I can help with that. I know where the bombs are planted to blow the tunnel. I am familiar with the location. Let me handle that. Chief Bruckhart and his men have already taken care of the canal, and they have left the area. As far as the powerstations, I can direct you. Powerstation No. 1 has three turbines. The bomb has been placed at the base of Turbine No. 2. It has the power to take out all three turbines.

"Now, Powerstation No. 2 has ten turbines. The bombs are placed at turbines numbered 2, 4, and 8. All the turbine numbers are clearly marked when you walk down between the two rows of turbines. Do you have a flashlight?"

"Yes. Fels was going to tell me how to disarm the bombs when he got here. What do we do?"

"All you need to do is turn off the alarm on the clock attached to each bomb. Then, to be sure, disconnect one of the wires from the battery pack likely next to the clock. It shouldn't matter which wire—just don't let it touch the other wire."

"It shouldn't matter?"

David smiled. "It will be fine. These are by no means sophisticated devices. Just handle them carefully, as they are equipped with very large charges. Disarm them all, then we can return and retrieve them afterwards.

"Now, it will take me some time to get down the tunnel. I do not know the exact locations of the tunnel bombs, but I do know generally where they are located. With the time it will take me to get down to the tunnel and disarm the bombs there, I will not be able to help you with the turbines. You will have to disarm all four of the bombs on your own. Start with Powerstation No. 2 first. It would be the greatest loss if we run out of time."

"I hope you're right about all of this." Blackmon looked at his watch. "Forty-eight minutes."

The two nodded at each other and quickly went their separate ways.

While David worked his way down to the head of the tunnel, Blackmon scrambled to Powerstation No. 2. He tried two doors; both were locked. He broke a window with the butt of his Colt and climbed into the building. The turbines were loud outside the building, but they were nearly deafening inside.

He had entered near the northeast end of the building. There were dim lights providing enough illumination that he could see where he was going. The turbine casings were located on the main level, so he could easily work his way around the base of the turbines. He would need his flashlight, however, to search for the bombs.

Standing near the entrance, he found himself facing a turbine. He saw the row of turbines lined up to the southwest toward the river. What he did not see was any indication of the turbine number. He wondered if David was wrong and if he would have to examine all ten turbines in the remaining thirty-nine minutes.

Blackmon made his way around the first turbine, looking for any sign of a number. As he got to the other side of the turbine, he was now between the two rows of turbines. Looking across the aisle to the turbine opposite of where he had entered, he saw a large number 1 painted on the side. He took a few steps toward Turbine No. 1, turned, and shone his flashlight up at the turbine he had passed. A large number 6 was painted on it. He turned around and rushed past Turbine No. 1. Next in line was Turbine No. 2. He had it figured out: Turbines 1 through 5 on one side, and turbines 6 through 10 on the other.

Blackmon looked at his watch. Thirty-three minutes, assuming the clocks on the bombs were set the same as his watch. He would have to move faster.

He ran to Turbine No. 2. The turbines themselves were contained within a blue housing. Blackmon estimated each one to be about 15 feet high and about 25 feet in diameter. There were vent holes all around the base, as well as four rows of vent holes from just above the base up to the top of the housing.

Blackmon felt as though the bombs would be placed at the base, or within a vent hole at the base. Anything placed in an upper vent hole would likely just fall to the bottom of the housing. Blackmon made his way around Turbine No. 2, looking for any indication of something placed at the base or within one of the base vents. He was looking closely, but trying not to take too much time. He was just over half way around the turbine—he had counted 19 vent holes—when he noticed something in a vent. Dropping to his knees, he closely inspected the hole.

What he saw were sticks of dynamite taped together in a bundle just large enough to fit in the vent. He examined the charge closely. He saw wires extending toward the next hole. There he saw more dynamite, but no clock. A third hole contained more dynamite, and finally he saw the clock in the fourth hole.

He examined the clock before making any attempt to disarm the bomb. The clock was taped to a battery pack with one wire running from the battery to the back of the clock. It appeared that the second wire on the clock was connected to the first bundle of dynamite. The other wire on the battery was also connected to the first bundle of dynamite. The alarm going off would complete the circuit and trigger the explosion.

He would need to turn the alarm clock around to turn off the alarm. The wires to the dynamite were stiff, creating a concern. He knew where the switch would likely be to turn off the alarm, but he could not risk trying to shut it off without seeing it.

He slowly moved the clock toward the dynamite sticks, bending the wires to create enough slack to turn the alarm clock around. The switch was where he had expected. He said a quick prayer as he moved the switch.

So far, so good. Now he had to remove one of the wires. He took the nearest wire in his hand and tightly gripped the clock. Another quick prayer as he gave the wire a quick tug. It came out of the opened back of the clock.

He was still alive. He curled the wire several times around his finger, and then let it dangle loosely. One down, and two to go ... in Powerstation No. 2. Then he would need to get to Powerstation No. 1.

He glanced at his watch while making his way to Turbine No. 8. Twenty-two minutes. He should have checked the time on the alarm clock. He'd do that at number 8.

Arriving at Turbine No. 8, Blackmon wasted no time in searching the vent holes at the base. This time, he went nearly the entire way around the turbine before he found the bomb. He kicked himself for not starting in the other direction.

CHAPTER 26

Fels desperately sought a way to loosen the ropes binding him to the wooden chair. Looking about in desperation, he realized he was surrounded by broken glass. He immediately threw himself sideways in the chair and crashed to the floor ... and into the deadly pool of flammable liquid.

His hands frantically searched and found a large shard of broken glass. Fels fiercely began sawing at the ropes around his wrists. It was an agonizingly slow and painful process as he worked on the ropes, and his fingers were sliced by the broken glass he was using. Blood dripped from his hands, mixing with the lethal liquid surrounding him.

Fels could hear the fire roaring in the back room as shelves and wooden crates ignited as if kindling for a bonfire. The room was already growing warmer as the fire licked at the outside of the office walls. He finally broke free from the ropes securing his wrists and hastily untied the bindings at his ankles.

He rose from the floor as fire penetrated the wall at the back of the room and rapidly consumed the tapestry hanging there. Fels leaped through the doorway into the hall where the fire was now rapidly approaching as it ate the liquid fuel poured out by Max. The heat was intense as Fels turned to the right and exited through the door into the tavern. He rapidly retreated out the front door as the building was engulfed in flames. He looked back, and momentarily, he saw his own home being consumed by the flames.

Fels ran the few blocks to where he had parked his motorcycle. Approaching the motorcycle, in one swift motion Fels mounted the machine, started it, and headed for the powerstations. He ignored the blood dripping from his hands and covering the grips of the handlebars. He had one focus—he hoped he could get there in time to help Blackmon. He had only traveled a block when he saw a man waving him down. It appeared to be David.

Fels stopped his motorcycle. "David! I was hoping I would see you sooner—"

"I know, but everything has been taken care of for you. The chief and his patrolman rounded up the group headed for the canal. But listen. Blackmon is disarming the bombs at Powerstation No. 2. I'll take care of the tunnel, but you will have to disarm the bomb at Powerstation No. 1."

"Fine. I know where it should be located. But will Blackmon be okay?"

"Some things are not mine to determine. Now go!"

"Hop on the back."

David tilted his head and smiled. "I can get there quickly enough. Go!"

Fels powered the motorcycle away as fast as he could.

Approaching Powerstation No. 1, Fels thought he saw a figure just off the roadway near the entrance to the facility. He stopped his motorcycle and approached on foot. The man saw Fels and began to run. Fels pursued him and ran him down in no time. He tackled him, wrestled him on to his stomach, and lifted his hands behind his back.

It was John Meno, the new man who had identified him to Max. As Fels held him to the ground, the man swore at Fels and blamed him for everything that had gone wrong in his life because of the arrest made by Fels. Fels removed a pair of handcuffs from under his coat and secured Meno to a nearby lamppost.

Returning to his motorcycle, Fels checked his watch. He only had eleven minutes to disarm the bomb. Fortunately, since he had seen the plans, he knew exactly where it was located.

He made his way into Powerstation No. 1. He moved quickly around the base of the turbine and located the bomb. He disarmed it as the time approached three minutes to detonation. He breathed a sigh of relief, but halted that reaction as he thought about Blackmon at Powerstation No. 2. Fels ran to the door.

At Powerstation No. 2, Blackmon had encountered a problem. He quickly located a bomb at Turbine 4, but there was only one set of taped dynamite sticks, unlike the three bundles wired together at the other two turbines. It didn't seem right to him, so he continued searching the vents. About a third of the way around from the first bomb, he found a second. In his mind, he knew right away that there would be a third. He only had two minutes remaining.

He disarmed the second bomb, then scrambled around the turbine, locating the third bomb. By his watch, he was already too late. He did not have time to disarm it according to plan. He reached in, grabbed the alarm clock, and pulled it quickly from the vent, disconnecting both wines as he did so. He looked up to see Fels running toward him as the alarm clock rang in his hand.

Blackmon looked at Fels in disbelief. "Powerstation No. 1! We're too late!"

"No, I took care of it."

"But I thought—"

"It's a long story."

"And I assume your friend David Smith disarmed the tunnel bombs?"

"Well, I haven't seen him, but I'm certain he handled it." Fels let out a delayed sigh of relief and enjoyed it for a moment. The two men exited the power station together.

"Listen to that, will you?" Fels said.

"What's that?"

"Why nothing but rushing water and spinning turbines in the still night air." Both men smiled.

As it did every day in the morning, the sun rose in the east. There were a few clouds in the mostly clear, lightening sky. It was a typically cold late November day, the day before the Day of Thanksgiving. Many people were already on their way to work. The electric street lamps that only moments before had been glowing were being turned off. Some shops had their lights on in the early morning, making ready for customers. The trolley cars were running. Everything was as normal as it could be.

Fels lifted himself off the couch where he had fallen asleep in his clothes. He was dirty, there was dried blood on his face and clothing, his hands felt the sting of the numerous fresh cuts. He stretched his tired body, rubbed his head, and stared at his hands held out in front of him.

His thoughts turned to his family. Not sad thoughts, but thoughts of the joy they must feel. Knowing they were in a far better place brought him a sense of peace. He went to the sink and washed his face and hands. The water stung his hands, but he knew he needed to keep the cuts clean. He had told the chief hours ago that he didn't need any medical attention, but the chief insisted that Fels see the doctor in the morning. Fels had to agree before the chief would let him go home.

Fels put on a fresh set of clothes after washing up. His face was bruised from where he had been hit several times by Max. He knew he would be fine, but he would keep his word to the chief and see the doctor. He put on his shoes, coat, and hat and exited the apartment building.

The streets were filled with people, all unaware of the events of just a few hours ago. They were on their way to work or shopping, and they were thinking of the feast of a turkey dinner that had become commonplace for the Day of Thanksgiving.

"You at least look cleaner, but you really don't look great."

Fels turned and saw David. "Gee, thanks for that keen observation, David." Fels looked up and down at David. "You seem to have no problem in looking fresh this morning." They smiled at one another.

"I suppose not, but that is just incidental to everything else. I just try to blend in as best as I can. How are you feeling, I mean really feeling deep down inside, in your heart?"

Fels felt David's concern. "I feel fine. I mean it. I thought of Marie and Ludwig and Frieda this morning. David, it was all joyous and peaceful thoughts. I can't tell you enough how thankful I am that you helped me to understand this. My heart feels the grace of God." Fels gave David a warm smile.

David extended his hand to Fels, and Fels gripped it tightly. "Fels, you will no longer feel a loss of your family, but rather a comforting closeness to them. It is all part of God's plan. It is nothing I have done; it is what you have accepted."

Fels shook his head and once again felt the warmth and peace that David exuded and that he selflessly shared. They slowly lowered their hands. The stare into David's comforting eyes seemed to last for minutes, and then David turned and disappeared into the mass of people moving along the sidewalk.

Fels wanted to ask David if he would see him again. Maybe it was best not to know. David had made it clear that Fels needed to rely on God and God alone. David was a messenger sent for a purpose. Had that purpose been fulfilled in Fels' coming to peace with the loss of his family? Perhaps, yet, David helped in other ways as well.

Fels stood on the sidewalk as the world passed by. He thought about purpose.

CHAPTER 27

Fels awoke from a sound sleep, still bruised, and still fully alive. He dressed and met Blackmon for breakfast. It had been three days since the two had stopped the bombing of the powerstations. They had a meeting scheduled with Chief Bruckhart later in the morning. They both wanted to talk before seeing the chief.

"So, everything's good at the BOI?" asked Fels.

"Well, yes. Agent Wilson made some fuss, but in the end we stopped a potential disastrous act of espionage by the Germans on American soil. While the official direction of the BOI is to keep its investigations into German activities limited, it appears we one-upped the Secret Service on this one. Of course, Agent Wilson tried to play up the cooperation between the two organizations, as a result of considerable effort on behalf of the Secret Service." They shared a smile. "The New York office understands the actual story. So, yes, all is good. How about on your end? Have you spoken to your chief, or is today's meeting your first?"

"No. I went in the day after the arrests. Chief Bruckhart is pleased at the final outcome. He had some reservations about getting the department involved, but he thanked me for my persistence."

"So, are you still on leave?"

"You know what, I had forgotten, but that ended on November 24th!" They laughed.

The two finished their breakfasts and walked to the 5th Precinct enjoying a cold, sunny morning. Both men were lost in their thoughts when Blackmon finally spoke. "What are your plans, Fels? Are you staying with the Tonawanda Police Department? You know, if the Buffalo BOI office is going to grow, we could use some good men from the area."

"Well, Myron, I've been giving that some thought, and I'm really not sure at this point. I want to see how our meeting goes today, but I have a sense that it may be time for me to move on. Just exactly what that means at this time, well ...."

"I understand. Just keep the BOI on your list of options."

The two smiled at one another as they rounded the corner to the 5th Precinct.

Chief Bruckhart had also invited Captain Flynn into the meeting. The four men sat around a table in the squad room.

Chief Bruckhart opened the meeting. "Thank you, Agent Blackmon, for taking the time to meet with us. I've asked Captain Flynn to sit in with us since he is Fels' direct superior in the department.

"Let me get to the point. The department owes a great deal of gratitude to the two of you for what you did. But, obviously, beyond that, the country owes you that gratitude. Unfortunately, the Secret Service is seeing that their agency wraps up this entire affair. They feel it is best for the country that the Secret Service was able to uncover the totality of the German espionage operation.

This has apparently been approved at the highest levels in Washington."

Fels scowled and then laughed. "That Agent Wilson is really something." He turned to Blackmon. "Were you aware of this, Myron?"

"Yes. The chief here asked me not to say anything about it, as he felt that was his job. I hope you understand, Fels."

"Oh, that's not a problem with me. My reward, after all, is knowing that the right thing was done and that the plot was terminated. And, I guess the Secret Service did handle a piece of the whole thing." He chuckled to himself. "We all did our part with the information we had. How about you, Myron?"

"Oh, I'm good. I've known from the start that the BOI's involvement in German affairs has always been limited. So, it's a non-issue for me. At the same time, as you know, the New York office is well aware of the full story. Chief, I hope you and your department can appreciate how this must be handled on a national level. But, know that the BOI is greatly thankful for what this department has done. I am certainly going to be coordinating efforts with the Tonawanda police in the future."

The comments of both men pleased Chief Bruckhart. "I know a mere thanks seems like so little, but truly thank-you, men.

"Of course, as you both know, Maximilian Strasse evaded capture. Agent Wilson shared with me that their tracking showed that he likely escaped to Mexico. It seems he was held with some esteem for his enterprising work to help the German espionage plans against America. They lost the trail in Mexico, but Agent Wilson thinks he may have disappeared in South America. We can only hope we have heard the last of the man."

The chief ended his comments on a rather somber note, but tried to lift the mood. He smiled at Fels, "Now,

Fels, about your leave. With all things considered, your leave has been removed from the books, and you will receive your full pay for your time off. We will see you back here Monday morning, bright and early!"

Myron gave Fels a congratulatory slap on the back, and Flynn told him he was happy to have him back, assuming he was healthy enough. They shook hands all around, and after some small talk among the men, Fels and Blackmon left the building together.

As they made their way along the sidewalk, Blackmon asked, "Okay, what about your options? Any revelations?"

Fels let out a deep sigh. "I don't feel certain about anything except that I know I need a change. I'm going to Turners for a work-out and some deep thinking."

The two shook hands as they went their separate ways at the end of the block.

Fels returned to work at the 5th Precinct. The men lauded him for his keen instincts and dedication to duty. Eventually, the unexpected undertakings were lost to the daily duties of everyone's assignments. Fels was pleased when more normalcy returned to his work as a detective. Still, he was nagged by that feeling that it was time to move on.

The war between Germany and Great Britain continued to heat up, and the opinions of Americans varied widely on whether or not America should enter the war. Even before war broke out, American opinion had been overall more negative toward the German Empire than toward any other country in Europe. Military considerations were seldom raised. In America, the decisive questions dealt with morality and visions of the future. The prevailing attitude was that America possessed a superior moral position as the only great nation devoted to the principles of freedom and democracy. America felt it could preserve those ideals, and eventually, the rest of the world would come to appreciate and adopt them.

Leaders of most religious groups promoted pacifism, as did leaders of the women's movement. The Methodists and Quakers, among others, were vocal opponents of the war. President Wilson, who was a devout Presbyterian, would often frame the war in terms of good and evil in an appeal for religious support of the war.

Then there was a group who called themselves the Atlanticists. They advocated for an enduring postwar alliance with Great Britain, which they saw as vital to maintaining America's future security. Supporters included former President Theodore Roosevelt, as well as several influential politicians and lawyers.

Moods shifted when several U.S. ships traveling to Britain were damaged or sunk by German mines. Last February, Germany announced unrestricted warfare against all ships, neutral or otherwise, that entered the war zone around Britain. On May 7, 1915, a German U-boat had torpedoed the passenger liner *Lusitania* off the coast of Ireland, killing 1,195 people, including 128 Americans. The German government maintained that the *Lusitania* was carrying munitions, but the U.S. demanded reparations and an end to German attacks on unarmed passenger and merchant ships.

In August, Germany had pledged to see to the safety of passengers before sinking unarmed vessels, but in November they sunk an Italian liner without warning, killing 272 people, including 27 Americans. With these attacks, public opinion in the United States began to turn irrevocably against Germany. These events appeared to Americans as an unacceptable challenge to America's rights as a neutral country, and as an unforgivable affront to humanity.

Fels was catching up on these events following the conclusion of his investigation into German espionage. He had not really had much opinion about America's involvement in a potential war until his entanglement in the plot to blow the American powerstations. He was now very aware of the German desire to bring America to its knees.

Fels struggled, trying to understand what, if any, role he should take in the current state of affairs. David had let him see his true spirit and the truth of God. He saw a path for himself in law enforcement and in peacekeeping. Was supporting war keeping peace? Was actually engaging in the war effort a way to keep peace by defeating the enemy who was seeking to destroy us? It had all seemed so clear when he was engaged in deep conversation with David, but now it was not so evident to him.

Finally, Fels did what he should have done first; he prayed about it. With a sincere heart, he reached out to God. Although he had the free will to do whatever he wanted, he needed clarity to make a decision. He prayed for weeks, but he just did not feel any new sense of direction. Still, he kept his faith and prayed without ceasing.

It was a Saturday morning, and Fels had gone to the diner in Amherst where he and Blackmon had met several times. He finished his meal and was enjoying another cup of coffee when Blackmon entered the diner. Seeing Blackmon enter, Fels waved to get his attention. Blackmon saw him and headed to the booth where Fels was sitting.

"Myron, good to see you! It's been awhile."

"Glad to see you, Fels. Yes, it's been a few months. I guess we've both been busy."

"Sit down. Do you have a few minutes to catch up?"

Blackmon slid into the booth. "Of course!"

Blackmon ordered breakfast, and they brought each other up to date on their current activities. Blackmon noted the BOI was considering opening a fully staffed and equipped field office in Buffalo. If that were to happen, Blackmon would be assigned as the Special Agent in Charge, the highest ranking criminal investigator in the region. In this position, Blackmon would report directly to the agency in Washington, D.C.

Fels shared with Blackmon his desire to move on. He had given himself four months to make a decision following the closing of the case. That mark had passed two weeks ago. He told Blackmon about his struggle with a nagging feeling about being involved in the potential war effort, especially as it appeared more and more likely that America would officially enter the war.

Blackmon disclosed some information to Fels about a developing intelligence service within the Army. While Great Britain had a formal organization, the United States had never formalized a dedicated organization specifically for intelligence. President Wilson had been opposed to espionage in general, but he recently realized it was necessary to build intelligence programs within the United States. The driving factor was that British intelligence had alerted President Wilson to the fact the Germans were infiltrating businesses, financial institutions, and government agencies.

Specifically, the U.S. agency was to be called MI-8, a label used by the British. Their mission would be to decode military communications and create codes for the U.S. military to use. It would require men with good minds, keen instincts, investigative skills, and a dedicated work ethic. As Fels had shared his concern about being a peacekeeper, Blackmon noted how the efforts of this agency would counter enemy activities against the United States. Blackmon thought it would be a perfect fit for Fels.

Fels listened intently. He found that the more he heard about the program, the more he was drawn into it.

Every sense told him that this was the direction he should take. Blackmon gave Fels the name and phone number of a contact. Blackmon finished his breakfast, and Fels thanked him for all of his support. They said their pleasantries, and Blackmon left the diner.

Fels reached over and picked up the check for their meals as he had insisted that he do. It was face up on the table. Fels looked it over to see what he owed. He noticed there was writing on the back of the bill. He turned it over and saw a brief note. It read, "And your ears shall hear a word behind you, saying, 'This is the way, walk in it.' Isaiah 30:21." It was signed by David.

Fels looked about the diner. There were only two other people finishing their breakfast. He hurriedly paid his bill and rushed out the door. He looked about on the busy street, but David was nowhere to be found.

FACT AND FICTION

THE BACKDROP OF THE HISTORICAL NOVEL

The heading of this section defines the historical novel as it is a mix of Fact and Fiction. As most openly defined, historical fiction describes any work of literature in which a fictional story occurs prior to the author's present time (according to writers.com/what-is-histori-cal-fiction). This source notes that this leaves a lot open to interpretation, depending upon both the writer's and the reader's age.

So, the consensus among most writers and readers is that, for a work to be "historical," it should be set at least 50 years prior to the year of publication. Additionally, the setting of the story needs to be culturally recogniz-able.

What this means is that the setting must be signifi-cant to history, recognizable by historians, and impact the plot of the story. An essential element of historical fiction is that it attempts to convey the spirit, manners, and social conditions of a past age with realistic detail and fidelity to historical fact.

In *Torrents*, the historical period is the early 1900s, just prior to America's entry into World War I. Research into this period meant looking at clothing styles, jobs, housing, transportation, and so much more. Further, I studied the geography of the novel using maps from that period. I used actual street names in the story.

Because the novel's main character is a police officer, I conducted a lot of research into how police departments in the areas around Buffalo, New York, were organized and managed in that era.

The location of Niagara Falls meant stepping back in time to see how the Niagara River was developed and used to power local mills, and to provide electric power to the area.

Now, I also did some online research that may have put me on some list somewhere. Searching for how to make a simple bomb in that time period, types of handguns used by the police, the FBI organization, the Mafia, and the bombing of the Welland Canal must have looked like a strange search pattern to someone!

So, let's get down to the story and the facts and fiction. The historical backdrop is the Buffalo, New York, area in the early 1900s. I set the story in this locale because of the facts of the attempts to sabotage the Welland Canal. More about that later.

THE SETTING OF WORLD WAR I

With my main character set, and with a general time frame of the early 1900s, I searched for a historic event in which to place the character. From my previous novel, *The Blacksmith*, I had an interest in the World Wars. So, this led me to look for espionage efforts by Germany near the beginning of World War I. References to World War I and the events leading up to it are, of course, nonfiction.

It is interesting to note that the MI-8 intelligence organization as referenced in the Chapter 27 was also real.

CHARACTERS

Felsen Krieger

I enjoy discovering characters for my books among photos and stories of my ancestors. Louis (Ludwig) C. Wendt, my great-grandfather on my maternal side, was the inspiration for Felsen Krieger. He was born in April 1850 or 1851 in Germany, and he came to this country in 1882 with his wife and three young children, settling in La Porte, Indiana. He did not become a United States citizen until 1913. His death in 1931 was ascribed to his health and his old age.

Louis C. Wendt, early 1900s

My great-grandfather's inspiration for Felsen Krieger came in the form of a photograph. I do not have a date for the photograph, but I would guess him to be in his late-fifties in age. In the photograph, Louis is dressed in wrinkled baggy pants, a dark suit coat and matching dark vest, no tie, and a dark fedora. Pinned on his vest is a star-shaped law enforcement badge.

Census records reveal that Louis was a night policeman, policeman, and watchman between 1900 and 1910. A note on the back of the picture indicates that, at the time of the photograph, he was one of three La Porte policemen.

I have no other information about his work in law enforcement. There are no other similarities to the main character of this book. The photograph simply inspired me to write a story about a policeman in the early 1900s.

Other Fictional Characters

All of the member's of Felsen's family are fictional. The names of all the police officers are fictional. The men involved in the plot to destroy the powerstations are all fictional, including Max. All other minor characters are fictional.

Non-Fiction Characters

Myron Blackmon was an actual BOI agent living in Lancaster, New York. The Buffalo office of the BOI opened prior to 1925, and the Special Agent in Charge was Myron F. Blackmon. He is listed in this position in the 1920 Federal Census, and his 1918 draft registration card identifies him as a Special Agent.

The Buffalo field office closed in 1929. According to the *Lancaster Enterprise* newspaper from October 23, 1947, Myron Blackmon "for 12 years was agent in charge of the Chicago and Buffalo Divisions of the Federal Bureau of Investigation (F.B.I.)" when it closed. This would imply that the office would have opened about 1917. As he was Special Agent In Charge when the office opened, he was likely a regular Special Agent prior to this. He made a good fit for someone for Fels to engage in his own investigation.

The actions of the character of Myron Blackmon in this book are totally fictitious.

The German Intelligence Organization

The few details and most of the characters surrounding the German espionage plans are true. Section 3-B was the actual designation of the military intelligence organization in Germany at the time. The German Ambassador to the United States, Count Johann von Bernstorff, located in Washington D.C., was actually a trained espionage agent. He was Germany's espionage and sabotage chief for the entire Western Hemisphere. To support his effort, he was assisted by Captain Franz von Papen, a military attaché in Mexico who transferred to the United States, Captain Karl Boy-Ed, naval attaché, and Dr. Heinrich Albert, the commercial attaché who was handling the finances for the sabotage operations. The character of Max Strasse is fictitious, developed only for the story.

PLACES

The Welland Canal

The most prominent event of German sabotage near the beginning of World War I was the Black Tom explosion in New York Harbor in 1916. But I wanted something a little less well-known. This is when I ran across the attempts to sabotage the Welland Canal.

The Welland Canal is a ship canal in Ontario, Canada, and is part of the St. Lawrence Seaway and Great Lakes Waterway. The canal traverses the Niagara Peninsula between Port Weller on Lake Ontario, and Port Colborne on Lake Erie, and was constructed because the Niagara River—the only natural waterway connecting the lakes—was not navigable because of Niagara Falls. The Welland Canal enables ships to ascend and descend the Niagara

Escarpment, and has followed four different routes since it opened in 1829.

There were three attempts to destroy the locks of the canal, taking place in 1841, 1900, and 1915. The timing of the 1915 attack was a good fit for the period of my story, but it was a very unsuccessful attempt.

The newspaper reports in Chapter 18 are taken from actual newspapers at the time of the 1915 Welland Canal attempted bombing. The names noted in the news reports are the names of real individuals involved.

The Niagara River Powerstations

This is where I decided to add a little more interest to the story. The fictional part of my story was to include a plot to destroy the electric generating powerstations along the Niagara River. Of course, my main character as a local police detective would become engaged in the efforts to prevent the destruction. He gets some support from a non-fictional character, Myron Blackmon.

On the American side of the falls, the first powerstation, Schoellkopf Power Station No. 1, was in operation from 1882 to 1904. Next was the Niagara Power Station No. 1, operating from 1895 to 1961. Schoellkopf Station No. 2 was operational from 1898 to 1921. Niagara Power Station No. 2 operation from 1904 to 1961. Finally, within the timeline of *Torrents*, Schoellkopf Power Station No. 3a operated from 1914 to 1961.

Jacob Schoellkopf was a very successful businessman who owned multiple tanneries in Niagara, Milwaukee and Chicago. He was also very successful in the business of milling flour. Schoellkopf realized the future in harnessing the power of Niagara was in the commercial production of electricity. He adapted this available electrical technology to his powerhouse turbines and one of the first hydro-electric generating stations in the world was born.

Jacob Schoellkopf died in 1903, and his sons took over the operation of the power business. In 1918, Schoellkopf's Hydraulic Power Company merged with the Niagara Falls Power Company owned by Edward Dean Adams. The Niagara Falls Power Company name was retained.

The history of these stations and the underground tunnels that routed the water from the Niagara River are truly fascinating. It is worth the time to do a bit of research, and if you are ever in Buffalo, you can visit the historic sites and tour an underground tunnel.

ORGANIZATIONS

BOI (Bureau of Investigation)

The BOI was the first iteration of what would become the FBI. It all started with a short memo, dated July 26, 1908, signed by Charles J. Bonaparte, Attorney General, describing a "regular force of special agents" available to investigate certain cases of the Department of Justice.

The new organization had no investigators to call its own except for one or two special agents who carried out specific assignments on behalf of the Attorney General. There was also a force of examiners trained as accountants who reviewed financial transactions.

When an investigator was sent to help a U.S. Attorney build a case, he usually borrowed operatives from the Secret Service. These men reported not to the Attorney General, but to the Chief of the Secret Service. Congress banned the loan of Secret Service operatives to any federal department in May 1908.

So, the Attorney General created his own force of investigators. The Attorney General quietly hired nine of

the Secret Service investigators he had previously borrowed and brought them together with another 25 of his
own to form a special agent force. This new group had its
mission—to conduct investigations for the Department
of Justice.

In March 1909, the Attorney General named this
force the Bureau of Investigation (BOI). When the Bureau was established, there were few federal crimes. The
Bureau of Investigation investigated violations of laws
involving national banking, bankruptcy, naturalization,
antitrust, peonage, and land fraud. Because the early Bureau provided no formal training, previous law enforcement experience or a background in the law was desir-
able.

It was in 1935 that the organization came to be
known as the Federal Bureau of Investigation (FBI).

Organized Crime

The references to the individuals involved in organized crime are real. The first real boss of Buffalo's Mafia
was Giuseppe "Don Pietro" DiCarlo. He was supported
by his top lieutenant, Benedetto Angelo "Buffalo Bill"
Palmeri. DiCarlo was an associate of Manhattan-based
Mafia boss of bosses Giuseppe Morello before his move
to Buffalo.

The Black Hand described was also a real organization.

Max Strasse/Strada and his recruits are all fictional
characters.

The Turnverein, or Turner Society

The Turner Society as referenced in the book is a real
organization, and the facts noted in the book are real.
The only exception is their provision of physical rehabili-

tation services. I read nothing to indicate that they provided such a service.

The organization is still around today. There is an operating Turner Society in Fort Wayne, Indiana, less than 50 miles from where we live.

ANGELOLOGY

I enjoyed researching angels. I found some different opinions on their organization and activities, but for the most part, the general discussions of hierarchies, positions, and duties are similar. I have certainly oversimplified much of the information on angels, as there are numerous volumes written on the subject. I tried to be as true to the Christian views of angels as possible.

Sources used included:

Angels: What the Bible Really Says about God's Heavenly Host, Michael S. Herser, Lexham Press, 2018. This is a superbly researched and excellent book on the topic. I highly recommend this book to anyone interested in the topic. It is detailed.

The Hidden Hand of God: Extraordinary Angelic Encounters, Guideposts Editors, 2001. As stated on the book jacket, "A powerful collection of the privileged moments when real people were touched by a courier of heaven."

Angels in the Bible: What Do We Actually Know About Them?, Wayne Grudem, Zondervan Academic, https://zondervanacademic.com/blog/biblical-facts-angels, 2017. This post is adapted from Wayne Grudem's video lectures on Systematic Theology, available through MasterLectures.

Angels, God's Ministering Spirits, J. Hampton Keathley, III, Bible.org, https://bible.org/article/angels-god's-ministering-spirits, 2004.

Heaven, Randy Alcorn, Tyndale Momentum, 2004. While not specifically about angels, this book is a great source on the theology of heaven.

Additionally, numerous Bible-based articles were read, mostly focusing on the hierarchy and orders of angels.

DAY OF THANKSGIVING

The U.S. Continental Congress proclaimed a national Thanksgiving upon the enactment of the Constitution. Yet, after 1798, the new U.S. Congress left Thanksgiving declarations to the states; some objected to the national government's involvement in a religious observance, and Southerners were slow to adopt a New England custom. A national Thanksgiving Day seemed more like a lightning rod for controversy than a unifying force.

On October 3, 1863, during the Civil War, President Abraham Lincoln proclaimed a national day of thanksgiving to be celebrated on Thursday, November 26.

The holiday was annually proclaimed by every president thereafter, and the date chosen, with few exceptions, was the last Thursday in November. President Franklin D. Roosevelt, however, attempted to extend the Christmas shopping season by moving the date back a week, to the third week in November. But not all states complied, and after a joint resolution of Congress in 1941, Roosevelt issued a proclamation in 1942 designating the fourth Thursday in November (which is not always the last Thursday) as Thanksgiving Day.

Source: *Britannica*, David J. Silverman, https://www.britannica.com/topic/Thanksgiving-Day, 2023.